PENGUIN BOOKS
TALES ONCE TOLD

Abraham Eraly is the author of two critically acclaimed books on Indian history, *The Last Spring: The Lives and Times of the Great Mughals* (1997) and *Gem in the Lotus: The Seeding of Indian Civilization* (2000). His novel, *Night of the Dark Trees*, was published recently.

Born in Kerala, and educated there and in Chennai, Eraly has taught Indian history in colleges in India and the United States, and was the editor of a current affairs magazine for several years.

He now lives in Chennai, and is working on a study of classical Indian civilization. He can be contacted at abraham_eraly@yahoo. co.in

Also by Abraham Eraly

Gem in the Lotus: The Seeding of Indian Civilization
The Last Spring: The Lives and Times of the Great Mughals
Night of the Dark Trees

TALES ONCE TOLD

Legends of Kerala adapted from
Kottarathil Sankunni's *Ithihyamala*

ABRAHAM ERALY

Illustrated by Jayachandran

PENGUIN BOOKS

An imprint of Penguin Random House

PENGUIN BOOKS

USA | Canada | UK | Ireland | Australia
New Zealand | India | South Africa | China | Singapore

Penguin Books is part of the Penguin Random House group of companies
whose addresses can be found at global.penguinrandomhouse.com

Published by Penguin Random House India Pvt. Ltd
4th Floor, Capital Tower 1, MG Road,
Gurugram 122 002, Haryana, India

First published by Penguin Books India 2006

Copyright © Abraham Eraly 2006
Illustrations copyright © Jayachandran 2006

All rights reserved

10 9 8 7 6 5 4 3 2

For sale in the Indian Subcontinent and Singapore only

ISBN 9780143099680

Typeset in Sabon by Mantra Virtual Services, New Delhi

Printed at Repro India Limited

www.penguin.co.in

Contents

For . . .
who touched me with a lucent hand
as our vagrant lives crossed,
and turned the roiling,
woeful night
froth with stars.
For one brief moment.

Preface

This book is based on the *Ithihyamala*, an eight-volume compilation of Kerala legends written in Malayalam by Kottarathil Sankunni in the early decades of the last century, between 1909 and 1934.

One of the most popular books ever published in Malayalam and a perennial bestseller, the *Ithihyamala* has in all 126 chapters, with several anecdotes in many of its chapters. From these, I have selected a small number of stories that particularly reveal the unique lifestyle and socio-cultural milieu of pre-modern Kerala.

These are not folktales, but historical anecdotes of a legendary character. Most of the events described in them lack hard historical veracity, but they are nevertheless invaluable for exploring the psyche of old Kerala lying beneath the surface clutter of manifest facts. The lost innocence of the people. The *Ithihyamala* deals with an age when life in Kerala was simple and rustic, its flow tranquil, and this is reflected in the very timbre of these stories, which have about them an air of artless credulity—of naivety, in fact. This is a major part of their charm.

But more than anything else, these are fascinating tales in themselves.

What I have attempted here is not a direct translation—the original stories are too rambling for that—but a retelling, by condensing the stories, and in some cases restructuring them or adding brief explanatory material, but without altering their tone and substance.

Twenty-one of these stories, in slightly different versions, were published by me under a pseudonym in *The Hindu* between 1997 and 1999.

Abraham Eraly
January 2006

There is something in the soil of Kerala, or perhaps in its air, that gives an irreverent and sardonic bent to the character of Malayalis. Not surprisingly, some of the most celebrated folk heroes of medieval Kerala were pranksters and wits. And among them, none had a better—or worse—reputation than Naduvelippat Bhattathiri, who once played a humiliating practical joke even on his guru, though gurus in India were generally revered by their disciples as next only to god.

Naduvelippat was at this time living in a Brahmin seminary in Thrissur in central Kerala, pursuing higher studies in the Vedas after completing his basic education at home. Though he was a keen student, he had a weakness for women, which was unbecoming in a youth of his calling. Oddly, the head of the institution, a Namboodiri, also had the same vulnerability, and maintained a concubine in the town, despite being a married man. The guru tried to keep the matter a secret, because such liaisons were forbidden to married Namboodiris, though unmarried adults of the community were free to have, were indeed expected to have, such affairs.

The Namboodiri was under the impression that no one knew of his infatuation, but of course everyone knew. And Naduvelippat took full advantage of it. Soon it became a nightly routine at the seminary for the guru to sneak out to visit his mistress after his wards had gone to bed, and for our young scholar to sneak out soon after, to go on his own jaunts. Naduvelippat had no regular concubine, but spent the night wherever fancy and opportunity took him, and he normally got back to the seminary early in the morning, well before the Namboodiri returned. But sometimes he would oversleep because of his nocturnal labours, and on such occasions he was often caught stealing back, and had to suffer the mortification of being roundly berated by the Namboodiri.

To avoid this embarrassment Naduvelippat took to going to the local temple straight from his tryst and spending some time there in worship, so that whenever the Namboodiri caught him, he could truthfully say that he had been to the temple. But one day he got involved in a caper, and could return to the hostel only late at night. That got him into serious trouble, for the Namboodiri, who had not gone to his mistress that night and was lying awake waiting for him, caught him sneaking in. This could not be allowed to go on, the Namboodiri decided. He had to enforce discipline.

'Hereafter you should sleep only beside my bed,' he sternly ordered. 'And you should not go to the temple in the morning for worship, but say your prayers sitting where you sleep.'

Naduvelippat meekly promised to obey the guru, but bided his time to find some means to free himself from the restrictions. That was not easy, for the Namboodiri now stopped visiting his concubine, feeling guilty that it was his own liaison that gave the youth the excuse and the opportunity for his escapades. The arrangement however did not last long,

for the guru fretted as much as the disciple under the new regimen. Eventually, after a few weeks of continence, the guru's ardour got the better of him, and late one night, after making sure that Naduvelippat was asleep, he quietly slipped out of the building and set out to his concubine's house.

But Naduvelippat was only pretending to be asleep. As soon as the guru left, he followed, and, taking a shortcut, reached the woman's house well before the guru, and hid himself near the door. When the Namboodiri arrived and called out to the woman, she opened the door and brought a pitcher of water for him to wash his feet. Taking advantage of this diversion and the darkness of that new-moon night, Naduvelippat quickly slipped into the house and hid under the woman's bed.

He did not get much sleep that night, but woke up well before dawn and began chanting sacred hymns, sitting near the bed on which the lovers were sleeping. That jolted the Namboodiri awake.

'Who's that?' he cried, startled.

'It's I,' said Naduvelippat humbly.

'You! What're you doing here?'

'Following your instructions,' said Naduvelippat.

'What?'

'Your order that I should lie only beside your bed and say my prayers on waking up—that's what I'm doing.'

'Enough! Enough!' growled the guru, and hurriedly got up to return to the seminary. Naduvelippat followed him, keeping a few mannerly paces behind. On the way the guru paused and turned to his disciple. 'Look, now on you can sleep wherever you want and go wherever you like,' he told him. 'I give you the freedom. But please don't harass me hereafter.'

'As you wish,' Naduvelippat submitted solemnly.

Naduvelippat never grew out of his mischievous ways, and took particular delight in deflating the bloated egos of the vain and the pretentious. One of his favourite targets later in life, while living in Thiruvananthapuram as a courtier of the raja of Travancore, was the prime minister himself, a plump and voluptuous dandy who was always dressed in a superfine, sheer dhoti fastened with an ornate and jewelled gold girdle. One day, seeing him ambling along in the palace compound, Naduvelippat approached him with a show of utmost respect, bending low and covering his mouth with a hand. The grandee looked down on him with disdain and asked sternly, 'What do you want?'

'A humble request,' Naduvelippat supplicated in a low voice.

'What?'

'May I kiss your arse, please?' he asked. 'Just once?'

The prime minister whirled away in anger, his face crimson, and hastened to the raja to report about the impertinence of Naduvelippat. 'This man is making my life miserable with his affronts,' he complained. 'Just now when I was coming here, he said something obscene to me, which I cannot even repeat to Your Majesty.'

When the raja summoned Naduvelippat and questioned him about it, he maintained that it was not true that he had insulted the prime minister. 'What happened is this,' he said. 'When I saw him dressed in a transparent dhoti and adorned with gold waist ornaments, I had a strong desire to kiss his plump bottom. It wouldn't have been proper for me to do that without his permission, so I asked him. I don't know why he is making such a fuss about it. If he didn't want me to kiss his bottom, all he had to do was to say so, and that would have been the end of the matter.'

The raja could barely suppress his smile, but dismissed Naduvelippat saying, 'I'll think over this matter and decide what to do. You may go now.'

The raja had never liked the prime minister going about in transparent clothes, but was at a loss about how to handle the matter tactfully. Naduvelippat's prank gave him an opening, and he now issued a general order making it mandatory for everyone to wear a second cloth around the waist while appearing in court.

Martial Arts Secrets

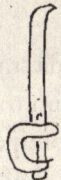

The priestly class in India, unlike in the Far East, did not normally practise the martial arts, but there were distinguished exceptions to this. Such is the story a Brahmin youth in north Kerala who took to kalaripayat, the unique martial arts of Kerala, and became renowned as Kallanthattil Gurukkal.

Gurukkal had his training under a prince of Kozhikode, himself a wizard in the art. One day, after a year of instruction, the prince asked the youth how many adversaries he could overcome if attacked.

'I can easily handle ten thousand,' boasted the youth.

And the prince said, 'Well, you have a lot more to learn.'

After another year the prince repeated the question, and this time the youth replied that he was confident of resisting five thousand. Again the prince said, 'You still haven't learned enough,' and continued the instruction. The following year the youth lowered the figure to two thousand, then lowered it again to one thousand the year after that, and so on year after year. Finally, after twelve years of training, he one day admitted that he was certain of subduing only one adversary.

As his skill grew, so did his humility.

This pleased the prince. Yet he was not fully satisfied.

'You have to train till your body becomes all eyes,' he advised.

'I don't understand,' said the youth.

'One day you will,' said the prince. 'Only then will you have become a true adept.'

So the youth continued his training for a couple of years more. Then the prince put him to a surprise final test.

Now, it was the youth's routine to sit in a walled enclosure and massage his body with oil after his daily workout. One day when he was thus engaged, the prince ordered two soldiers to secretly take up positions outside the door of the enclosure and, when the youth came out, to strike him suddenly with spears from both sides.

As the spears struck the youth, instantaneously, in the wink of an eye, he leapt away. When the prince, who was standing nearby, examined the spearheads he found a slight smear of oil on them but the youth did not have even a scratch on him. The disciple had passed the ultimate test.

'This is what I meant by the body becoming all eyes,' said the prince. 'Your body reflexes should be like the blinking of the eye when something is about to strike it. There should be no conscious thinking—the body itself should think, instinctually. And act instantaneously. You understand?'

'I do, sire,' said the youth. 'And I think I've acquired that skill.'

'Well then, your training is complete,' said the prince.

A few days later the youth presented the guru a suitable dakshina—a disciple's formal gift offering—and with his blessing set out to seek fame and fortune. Initially he served various local chieftains for some years, but finally arrived at the court of Raja Marthanda Varma, an early eighteenth century king of Travancore ruling from Padmanabhapuram in southern Kerala. The time of his arrival was opportune, for the raja was at that time looking for a skilled martial arts guru to train his heir, Prince Rama Varma. So when he was told that a Brahmin youth claiming to be a kalaripayat expert wished to have an audience with him, the raja decided to test him first, and told his officers to ask Gurukkal to come the next day at noon.

But when Gurukkal arrived at the royal fort at the appointed time, he found all the gates closed. Realizing that this was a test of skill that the raja had set for him, he confidently girded his loins and, taking a few crouching kalari steps, leapt over the fort wall, bearing his sword and shield. But he had underestimated the raja. The test was more hazardous than he had expected, for when he was about to land inside the fort, he noticed that several rows of spikes had been planted on the ground all along the wall, to impale intruders jumping into the fort. Seeing this, he instantly swung the shield under his feet and so landed safely on the spikes. Then, using the very momentum of the fall, he sprang right back over the wall to land safely outside the fort.

The raja, who was watching all this from a palace window, then had Gurukkal brought to him, congratulated him on his skill and appointed him as the prince's instructor. After some years, when the prince completed his training, the raja decided to test his skill, in very much the same manner in which the prince of Kozhikode had once tested the skill of Gurukkal. One day when he was on the top floor of the palace, and the prince was coming up the stairs to see him, the raja placed himself out of sight and struck at the prince's neck with his sword the moment his head appeared above the floor. Instantly, as the sword grazed the skin of his neck, the prince flung himself away and saved himself.

Later, when Gurukkal asked the raja why he had done such a rash thing, he said: 'I was testing him. He may have to face similar dangers from enemies, and I wanted to make sure that he has the skill to survive them. If he does not have the skill, he would be unfit to be the king.'

Gurukkal served the Travancore dynasty for many decades and prospered, and he brought his family from north Kerala and settled them in the southern town of Thiruvalla, where he had acquired extensive properties. His descendants also served as raja-gurus, and the office became hereditary in the family. However, in early modern times the family lost its kalari tradition, as the rajas of Travancore gave up practising the martial arts, and kalaripayat itself virtually died out in Kerala.

Mystery of a Miracle Cure

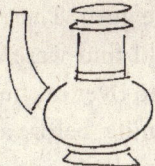

Once upon a time, many generations ago, there lived in Kozhikode, the capital of Malabar, a renowned visha-vaidyan, a physician who specialized in treating snakebite, a major cause of death in that serpent-infested region. Abiding by the conventions of his profession, the vaidyan never charged any fees for his services, nor accepted any payment voluntarily offered by his patients. Still, he managed to amass quite a fortune over the years, as grateful patients usually presented him gifts on some pretext or other.

Now there lived, in a mud and wattle hut adjacent to the physician's mansion, a poor labourer, and this man had a son named Kochu-Raman. The boy was a simpleton, but he dreamed of becoming a physician, rich and famous like his neighbour. So one day he approached a disciple of the vaidyan, told him of his fancy, and asked him what he should do to become a physician. The disciple, amused by the boy's ludicrous ambition, told him that all he had to do was offer a dakshina to the vaidyan and request him to accept him as a disciple. 'He will then give you a secret mantra,' said the disciple, 'and you should recite it with devotion as many

lakh times as there are syllables in it.' This would, the boy
was assured, fully qualify him as a physician, and he could
thereafter treat patients by sprinkling on them water or sacred
ash over which he had recited the mantra.

Kochu-Raman was delighted to hear that it was so easy
to become a physician. But he had a problem—he had nothing
to offer as dakshina to the guru. There were no valuables or
cash at home. All he could find were a couple of pumpkins
on the vine that had spread over his hut. These would do, he
decided. So early one morning, before anyone else had woken
up, he plucked the pumpkins and carried them to the
vaidyan's house and waited at his door. As soon as the
vaidyan opened the door, Kochu-Raman placed the pumpkins
at his feet and bowed low with his palms joined devoutly.

'What's this for?' asked the puzzled vaidyan, pointing to
the pumpkins.

'I wish to learn the mantra to cure snakebite,' said the
boy. 'Please teach me.'

'But why, *viddi, kushmandam*?' asked the vaidyan
testily—but why, idiot, the pumpkin?

Kochu-Raman could not understand what the vaidyan
was saying, but he in his nervousness and anxiety took the
words *viddi kushmandam* to be the secret mantra. So, seeing
the stern demeanour of the vaidyan and thinking that the
instruction was over, he touched the guru's feet reverentially
and hurried back home. He then took a ritual bath and,
sitting cross-legged on the floor before a lighted oil lamp,
recited the mantra five lakh times, as it had five syllables.
When he finished, he rose, firmly believing that he had indeed
become a visha-vaidyan.

There is an old saying in Kerala that visha-vaidyans and
serpents had a pact between them, by which snakes agreed

not to go out of their way to bite people, and vaidyans agreed not to go out of their homes to treat those bitten. Patients had to be taken to physicians for treatment. Visha-vaidyans were also forbidden to accept any fees for treatment. But Kochu-Raman did not know these conventions. So whenever he heard of a case of snakebite, he hastened to treat the victim, and he accepted whatever fees were offered. Often his mantra cure worked. Gradually his reputation spread, and he prospered. He then shifted to another part of the town and built a house of his own.

As matters were thus progressing, the Zamorin raja of Kozhikode was one day bitten by a snake, and though many visha-vaidyans, including Kochu-Raman's guru, were brought to treat him, none could revive him. On the third day, all hope was given up, and the raja was taken down from his bed and laid on the floor in preparation for the last rites. Then someone thought of Kochu-Raman and sent a palanquin to fetch him.

On his arrival Kochu-Raman made a show of examining the raja, then called the palace cook and asked him to prepare a bowl of rice gruel. When asked why, he replied that as the raja had not taken any food for two or three days, he would be hungry when he recovered and would ask for gruel. Hearing this, the attending physicians smirked covertly, for they considered Kochu-Raman a quack and the raja was as good as dead.

But Kochu-Raman was not perturbed. He called for a bowl of water, muttered his mantra 108 times over it and sprinkled the water on the raja's face. Presently, the raja opened his eyes. Again Kochu-Raman recited the mantra and sprinkled the water. Now the raja began to stir. And when a third time the water was sprinkled, the raja sat up and, as

Kochu-Raman had foreseen, asked for a bowl of gruel.

After eating the gruel the raja rested for a while. He then called Kochu-Raman to him and honoured him with a pair of hero-bracelets, presented him 10,000 gold coins and ten measures of silk as his fee, and had him carried to his house in a ceremonial procession, led by the royal band and escorted by the royal guards. Royal physicians also went along with the procession, wondering about the occult powers of the young visha-vaidyan. And among them was Kochu-Raman's unwitting guru.

In the rush of events at the palace, Kochu-Raman had not noticed his guru, but on his way home he saw him in the crowd following him. He immediately got down from the palanquin and went up to the guru, and placed at his feet all the gifts he had received from the Zamorin, saying that everything he had achieved in life was due to his advice and blessing.

'My advice?' asked the astonished guru. 'I don't remember giving you any advice. I was in fact going to ask you to teach me the spell to revive the dead.'

'The only spell I know is the secret mantra you taught me,' said Kochu-Raman.

'What mantra?'

'*Viddi kushmandam*,' whispered Kochu-Raman in the guru's ear.

Lenders Beware!

'In money matters you shouldn't trust anyone,' Thirumulpad said gravely. He was speaking to a poor old Brahmin who had brought his life's savings to deposit with him for interest. Thirumulpad, a rich landlord of Cherthala, was in the business of taking deposits and lending money, and he insisted that the Brahmin should take a bond from him for the money he deposited.

'It's not that I don't trust you . . .' began the Brahmin apologetically.

'Sentiment has no place in this matter,' said Thirumulpad. 'Whoever it is you are dealing with, you should make sure that the documents are all in good order.'

Thirumulpad was initially reluctant to accept the Brahmin's deposit. 'It will be a lot of bother for me to accept your deposit,' he said. 'I in turn will have to lend your money to someone else to earn interest on it, so I can pay interest to you. I may not find a good borrower. I may have to file a case to recover the money. But whatever happens, I will have to pay interest to you, and return your capital when you demand it. It's not worth the trouble.'

Still the Brahmin pressed Thirumulpad to accept the deposit. He had with him a thousand rupees, which he had carefully squirrelled away over a lifetime of humble work, mostly as a cook. 'I'm now too old to work,' the Brahmin said. 'And my children are not old enough to start earning. So we have to live on the interest of this money. I'm afraid to entrust it to anyone else.'

Thus pressed, Thirumulpad reluctantly agreed to accept the deposit. But he said he would give only sixty rupees as annual interest on the deposit. 'I'm doing this only to help you,' he said. 'But if you can find someone else to take the money for higher interest, I would suggest that you give it to him.'

The Brahmin was disappointed with the interest rate offered. But he felt that at least his money would be safe with Thirumulpad, so he deposited it with him and took a bond. And when the Brahmin called on him at the end of the first year, Thirumulpad promptly gave him the interest due.

This went on for five or six years without any hitch, but when the time approached for the bond to be renewed, Thirumulpad said that he did not want to keep the deposit any further. 'The bond expires tomorrow. I'll pay the interest and return your capital tomorrow morning,' he said. 'I'm short of the amount owed to you by about hundred rupees. I've five hundred rupees due to me as interest from someone, which he said he will bring early morning tomorrow, then I'll pay you.'

The Brahmin tried to persuade Thirumulpad to keep the funds, but he refused. 'Give it to someone else,' Thirumulpad advised. 'If you take property as security, you'll have nothing to worry about.'

On the invitation of Thirumulpad, the Brahmin spent the night in his house. The next morning at about 8 a.m., Thirumulpad said to him: 'The man who promised to bring the money has not yet come. I'll go and find out what's happening. Please have your meal by the time I return, so you can go straight back home without having to stop anywhere on the way to eat. It's not safe to stop on the way when you're carrying money. You can't trust anyone these days.'

So the Brahmin took his meal and waited. When Thirumulpad did not return even by 2 p.m., he began to worry. If the bond was not renewed that day it would lapse. He could maintain its validity only by filing a case, but this too had to be done that day itself. And he had to go to the district court in Alapuzha to file the case, and it was already too late for that.

While he was thus fretting, Thirumulpad returned. 'I've been running around all this time to get the money,' he said. 'I've managed to get it, though. But first let me go and have a bath and eat. I haven't eaten all day.' An hour later, he came to the Brahmin, and said, 'Why don't you spend the night here today and leave tomorrow morning? It's not safe to travel at night with money.'

That was prudent advice, the Brahmin thought. Early next morning Thirumulpad came to the Brahmin and said, 'Alright, let me settle your business. Give me the bond.' But on examining the bond he said, 'I'm sorry, this bond has lapsed. I can't give you money for this. No one pays on a time-lapsed bond.'

The Brahmin thought he was joking. 'Come on,' he said. 'You're joking.'

'I'm not joking,' Thirumulpad said sternly. 'I don't joke about money matters. I'll not pay on this bond. That's certain.'

Taken aback, the Brahmin pleaded with him for a while, but to no avail. He finally left the house, weeping and cursing his fate. Only god could help him now, and with that thought in mind he went to the Étumanur temple, to seek divine redress. As the Brahmin began his prayers there, Thirumulpad's body began to burn as if it was smeared with chilli paste, and his suffering increased with each passing hour. As he could find no relief from any medication, an oracle was called in, and he said that the affliction was caused by the anger of god for cheating a Brahmin, and that he would have relief only if the money was returned to the Brahmin and an equal amount donated to the temple. When this was done, he had immediate relief. And it cured him of his avarice too.

The Other Woman

It was a common and accepted practice in medieval Kerala for Brahmins, particularly Namboodiris, to form stable but not binding liaisons with women of the lower castes, especially with Nair women. The custom was called sambandam, and it developed out of a social need, for in Namboodiri families only the eldest son was usually allowed to marry within the caste and live with his wife at home. His brothers had to take women from other castes. But caste rules did not permit Namboodiris to marry Nair women and take them home. Nor could they go and live with them, but only spend the nights with them.

Nair women suffered no social stigma from such relationships, for marriage among them in pre-modern times was a mere formality, performed only to celebrate the attainment of puberty in girls. The bride usually did not cohabit with the man who tied the thali (the wedding pendant) on her, and they had no claims on each other. The marriage was merely symbolic, the groom a surrogate. Sometimes there was not even a groom; a sword substituted for him and the girl's mother tied the thali. After the ceremony, the girl was free to accept as lover any man of her choice, provided he was not of a lower caste. Usually the approval of the head of the family was sought to begin such a relationship, and sometimes there was a ceremony associated with sambandam, though it was not obligatory. The affair could be casual and temporary, or exclusive and long-lasting.

It was a familiar sight in Kerala villages till the early twentieth century to see men at dusk going to spend the night with their wives, and at dawn returning to their own homes. The sambandam system was an elegantly romantic arrangement, in which husband and wife remained lovers. And if they ceased to be lovers, they separated, without rancour or trauma, and without causing any disruption in the family. Their separation did not disturb family stability, for traditional Nair society was matrilineal, so married women did not move in with their husbands, but remained in their own homes. And the children born to a woman out of her liaisons took the caste and family name of their mother and lived with her in her home.

The arrangement ideally suited the old world, and provided absolute material and psychological security to women and children. And inter-breeding improved the genetic quality of the people. But the practice could exist only in an agrarian society and in a joint family setting. With the emergence of modern industrial society and the nuclear family, the sambandam system disappeared altogether.

Traditionally, Nair families considered it a high honour for their women to have Brahmin lovers. And Brahmins in turn considered it prestigious to have liaisons with women of aristocratic Nair families.

Married Namboodiris were not, however, allowed to have such affairs. But the rule was often flouted, and this at times created problems. Such was the case of a Thampuran (nobleman) of Edappally in central Kerala, who, though married, kept a concubine in Kalluppara, a nearby village, and took to living in the village to be near her, only occasionally visiting his ancestral home. It is doubtful whether he had ever slept with his wife or even seen her face after their marriage.

His wife suffered the neglect with quiet dignity and never once complained about it, so no one knew of the true state of their marriage. But it troubled the Thampuran's relatives that no heir was born to him even after some twelve years of marriage and his line was in danger of becoming extinct. They thought that the problem lay in his wife's barrenness. So after much discussion, a group of them went in a delegation to Kalluppara to appeal to the Thampuran to take a second wife.

Reluctantly he agreed, but raised an objection: 'To take a second wife I need the consent of my first wife. How can we get it? I won't ask her.'

The relatives then took on themselves the responsibility of securing the required permission. Returning to Edappally, they informed the Thampuran's wife of their mission, and appealed to her to permit her husband to take a second wife for the sake of the family's future.

She readily agreed. 'It's essential for him to have a son. That's my desire too. So I accept your proposal,' she said, but went on to add: 'But I've to caution you about one thing. You must check the girl's horoscope carefully before arranging the marriage. It'll do no good if her chart is like mine. She should have the good fortune to be able to conceive in Edappally when the Thampuran lives in Kalluppara.'

When the men returned to Kalluppara and informed the Thampuran of what transpired, he was crestfallen that his wife had unmasked him. But he also felt admiration for her acumen and wit, and the discreet manner in which she had let the truth be known. That shamed him into mending his ways. Soon he shifted to Edappally, never again to return to his concubine. Within a year a son was born to the couple, and the family, as in a fairy tale, lived happily ever after.

A Physician's Tale

For many centuries, the leading practitioners of Ayurveda in Kerala were the Ashta-vaidyans, patriarchs of eight families of hereditary Namboodiri physicians. They were, according to legend, invested with that privilege and responsibility by Parasurama, the mythical hero who raised the land of Kerala from the ocean. One of the most renowned of these physicians was Vayaskara Achan Moossad of the mid-nineteenth century. Moossad's treatments were often unconventional, sometimes even bizarre, but invariably effective. Blessedly intuitive, he was unerring in his diagnosis, and his healing hand—and the total faith of patients in his curative powers—worked wonders, however odd and seemingly trivial his prescriptions.

The most unusual story about Moossad is the way he cured a woman who was unable to lower her right hand that she had one day raised to take down a vessel from an upper shelf in her kitchen. Different physicians diagnosed the case differently—some said that it was a form of catalepsy, others diagnosed it as paralysis, and yet others claimed that possession by an evil spirit was the cause—but the treatments and rites they prescribed had no effect whatever. So finally her husband took her to Moossad.

When the woman was brought to him, Moossad was sitting in the veranda of his house attending to a crowd of patients who had gathered in the courtyard there. After examining her, he told her husband to tie her free left hand with a rope to a rafter of the veranda. And as she thus stood helpless before the crowd, Moossad asked the husband to pull off the dhoti around her waist, the only garment she was wearing. When the woman flinched and the husband hesitated, Moossad got up impatiently from his chair saying, 'Well, if you are unwilling, I'll do it myself,' and tugged at her dhoti. Instantly the woman brought down her frozen right hand to hold on to her dhoti, crying, 'Ayyo! Don't!'

Also typical of Moossad was the treatment he once prescribed for a man suffering from the blockage of the excretory passages and was unable to pass faeces or urine, and had been given up as incurable by several other physicians. As a last resort, a relative of the patient was sent to consult Achan Moossad. When the man arrived, Moossad was in the kitchen wing of his house, supervising servants dicing vegetables. On being apprised of the ailment, he took a pumpkin from the pile of vegetables, broke off its stem and gave it to the messenger, telling him to grind it in hot water and give it to the patient. On returning home, the man cut the stem into two halves, ground one half into a paste, mixed it in hot water, and gave it to the patient. Relief was almost immediate. Unfortunately, the patient then developed acute diarrhoea, so once again his relative rushed to consult Moossad.

'Did you use all the medicine I gave?' asked Moossad.

'Only half,' said the man.

'Give the rest also,' said Moossad. 'That'll fully cure him.' And it did.

Similarly, when a man who was so enormously fat that he could neither sit nor walk, was brought to him for treatment, Moossad examined him carefully and said: 'There is no use in treating you. The signs of death are on you, and you will die within thirty days. If by the grace of god or the strength of your life-force you survive, come again, and I will treat you.'

That sent the man into acute depression, as Moossad's diagnosis was never known to err. For many days thereafter he could not sleep, nor eat anything, except a little rice gruel once a day. Consequently, he lost weight rapidly and in a couple of weeks was almost reduced to skin and bones. But he did not die. So when the thirty-day deadline passed, he went to see Moossad again, as he had been asked to do.

And Moossad said to him: 'I warned you that you would die in a month not because I expected you to die, but only to make you grieve and thus lose weight. There is no treatment in Ayurveda for obesity. And now that you have become lean, you need no other treatment. But you have to take care not to put on weight again. Do vigorous exercise regularly till you sweat profusely—that's essential for good health.'

Equally odd was his treatment of a woman who had difficulty in childbirth. Even after four days of labour, she could not deliver the baby, but on the fifth day, the hand of the baby appeared through the vagina. On this unusual occurrence, the woman's husband went to consult Moossad. He pondered over the problem for a while, and then told the man to take a penknife or some such metallic thing, heat it red-hot, and jab the baby's protruding hand with it. This seemed to the man to be a horrible thing to do, but as the lives of the mother and her baby were at risk, he decided to try it anyway. The moment the hand was touched with the hot iron, the baby withdrew the hand, and in a short time the mother delivered the child without any complications.

Trial by Ordeal

At the court of Kulasekhara Varma, a ninth century Perumal ruler of Kerala, there was once a renowned satirical poet known only by his nickname, Tholan-kavi. His real name, family and place of birth are not known, though there is a popular belief that he was born in Eranikulam village in central Kerala. His poems are among the earliest works in Malayalam literature.

It was a teenage affair that earned the poet his strange and derogatory nickname, which was derived from thol, the inch-wide sash of leather that a Namboodiri boy had to wear on his left shoulder during his brahmacharyam (religious studentship), from the age of about seven, when his upanayanam (initiation ceremony) was held, till he was about sixteen, when he completed his obligatory studies and performed the samavarthanam rite to mark his adulthood.

Now, Brahmin boys, as brahmacharis, were expected to lead an austere and celibate life, but Tholan violated the code by having an affair with a maidservant of his mother. Though it was the woman who seduced him, the sin of weakness was on Tholan, and custom required him to atone for it by performing expiatory rites. But Tholan neglected to do that, for there was no one to guide him in this matter, as he had lost his father in his childhood and was living alone with his mother. Besides, he was a wild youth, indifferent to social conventions. Consequently, the elders of his community ostracized him, and when he came of age, they refused to perform his samavarthanam ceremony. He therefore had to unceremoniously remove the sash himself. But since he did not go through the customary rites, he was deemed to be still wearing the thol, and people took to derisively calling him Tholan. Later, when he became known as a kavi (poet), they called him Tholan-kavi.

Tholan-kavi couldn't care less about what people thought of him or what they called him. He had no tolerance for sham and pretence, and had once even dared to mock the literary affectations of the king, his patron. His acerbic tongue also antagonized several powerful courtiers, and they waited for a chance to get even with him. So one day when the raja lost his signet ring, they joined together and accused the poet of the theft. Tholan stoutly denied the charge, but the raja decided that the issue should be settled through a trial by ordeal, for the prevailing custom was that if a suspect refused to confess the crime he was charged with, he should prove his innocence by undergoing an ordeal.

The royal verdict was that the poet should dip his hand into a vessel of boiling ghee—if he was unscathed by that, he would be declared innocent, but guilty if he suffered burns. Tholan-kavi readily agreed to go through the trial. A fireplace was then set up in the palace courtyard and a pot of ghee placed on it. When the ghee came to a boil, an officer took it down from the fire using a potholder, and placed it before the raja. The raja then asked Tholan-kavi to go through the ordeal.

'That's not necessary,' said Tholan. 'We already know who is guilty.'

'What do you mean?' asked the raja.

'The officer who took down the vessel from the fire is the guilty one,' said Tholan. 'Otherwise why would he have needed a cloth to protect his hands?'

The answer confounded his accusers, and the raja had to set him free. But later they brought yet another charge against him, and again the raja ordered a trial by ordeal, this time ruling that Tholan should jump into a pond of crocodiles. Again Tholan agreed. At the appointed hour, as the raja and the courtiers assembled at the pond, Tholan arrived there with two newborn puppies, and wordlessly threw them into the pond. The reptiles immediately devoured them.

Tholan-kavi then turned to the raja and said: 'These puppies had barely opened their eyes after birth, so they could not possibly have committed any sin. Yet the crocodiles killed them. Evidently these creatures cannot distinguish between the innocent and the guilty. They will kill and eat whatever falls to them. Wouldn't they kill me too, though I am innocent?'

Again his adversaries were stymied. And they left him alone thereafter. 'These tricks of yours will work only on fools, not on a man like me,' Tholan warned them.

～

The Raja and the Magician

Kerala had at one time the dubious reputation of being the land of witchcraft, sorcery and magic. The speciality of the wizards of the region was in creating grand illusory spectacles, and no one had ever been better at it than Kaipuzha Thampan who lived at the turn of the eighteenth century.

One of Thampan's most sensational magic shows was performed at the royal palace in Thiruvananthapuram on a sweltering summer afternoon. He had on that day called on the raja to pay his respects, and the raja asked him, 'Have you any new tricks to show?'

'I don't have the skill to perform before Your Majesty,' demurred Thampan, 'and what little I've learned I've already shown here.'

'That's what you said last time also,' reminded the raja. 'Don't give any excuses now.'

'Your command!' submitted Thampan. 'But please, let's wait till it gets a little cooler.'

The raja agreed.

'God! How hot it is! It seems that the monsoon is going to be late this year,' he said. 'What do you think? How are

Mercury and Venus positioned?'

Thampan, who was also an expert astrologer, thought for a moment, then said: 'Doesn't matter where the planets are. It'll rain today.'

'Today?' laughed the raja. 'Impossible. There is absolutely no sign of it, not even a wisp of cloud.'

'I've no power to argue with Your Majesty,' said Thampan. 'But rain doesn't need any sign; it comes when it pleases. And it will come today.'

No sooner had Thampan said this than great thunderclouds were seen rolling over the western horizon from across the sea, heralding the monsoon. A cool breeze set in. Thunder rumbled in the distance.

'Amazing!' said the raja. 'Your prediction is coming true.'

The raja then moved from the royal chamber to sit in the portico of the palace to enjoy the welcome cool breeze. Presently it started to rain, and so heavily that the tank of the nearby Padmanabhaswamy temple began to overflow, with water entering the neighbouring houses and covering the palace compound.

'What shall we do now?' asked the perplexed raja. 'Water might even enter the palace.'

'It's all in the hands of god,' said Thampan.

Soon water rose up to the floor of the palace, and still continued to rise, causing considerable anxiety to the raja. But relief was at hand. A large, eighteen-oared barge commanded by a royal officer sped through the floodwaters and pulled up at the portico.

'Your Majesty must hurry,' said the officer. 'It's dangerous to remain here.'

'Come on, Thampan,' called the raja. 'Let's save ourselves.'

As the raja was about to step into the boat, Thampan checked him.

'Your Majesty, what are you doing?' he remonstrated.

'Why are you holding me back?' protested the raja, turning to Thampan. 'We'll all drown if we don't get into the boat.'

'Where's the boat?' asked Thampan.

As the raja turned around, the boat had vanished. There was no flood, no rain, no clouds in the sky. Instead, the sun was beating down mercilessly as usual. The storm was an illusion created by Thampan.

'You had me rather scared,' said the raja chuckling. 'Excellent! Excellent! I'm pleased.'

This was a private performance, so the raja asked Thampan to present a public show the next day. For this, Thampan spread a blanket in the courtyard of the main palace and began preparations for the show, and a large number of people gathered to watch him. But just then a thick rope with a piece of paper tied to it descended from the skies over the head of Thampan. He took the paper and, having read it, went over to the raja. 'I can't continue the show today, Your Majesty. I'm summoned to the heavens urgently,' he said, and handed over the paper to the raja. The paper, which was a letter from Indra, the king of gods, and bore his signature and seal, was written in Sanskrit, and it stated that war had broken out between gods and demons, and that Thampan should immediately rush to the aid of the gods.

With the king's permission Thampan then climbed the rope and disappeared into the skies. A while later, a rain of blood began to fall from the heavens, followed by a hail of dismembered human limbs, severed heads and headless corpses, as well as many dead bodies of elephants and horses, and finally the severed head of Thampan himself. Though everyone knew that all this was an illusion created by Thampan, the sight was too gruesome for many to bear, and the raja's mother, who was watching the scene from behind a screen, fainted. As the raja turned to attend to her, he heard Thampan calling him back, saying, 'No need to be perturbed any more. Today's show is over.'

As the raja looked back, the gory scene had disappeared, and Thampan was standing exultantly in the courtyard, surrounded by the gawking crowd.

Vararuchi, the renowned scholar-grammarian of ancient India, is said to have spent many years in Kerala in self-exile, out of shame for marrying a low-caste woman by mistaking her to be a Brahmin. During his travels in Kerala, the woman bore him twelve sons, but all were abandoned right after their birth wherever they were born, usually in a thicket along the road on which they travelled.

'Does the child have a mouth?' Vararuchi would call out to his wife from the roadside each time she delivered a baby.

'Yes,' the woman would answer from the thicket.

'Then leave it there,' he would direct. 'God who gave the child a mouth would also provide him food.'

Luckily, eleven of the infants survived, each rescued by a person of a different caste, and they all grew up to attain eminence in their particular caste vocations. And around their lives were woven many folk legends.

This is the story of Chathan, one of the sons of Vararuchi, who served as an attendant of Akavoor Namboodiri. The Namboodiri was a noble-minded and devout gentleman, but he once got entangled in a forbidden liaison with a low-caste

woman. This was not a happy affair, for the Namboodiri
was racked by awful feelings of guilt about it. Finally,
overcome with remorse, he ended the affair and set out on
an expiatory pilgrimage, taking Chathan along with him.
On this journey, Chathan, intending to teach his patron a
lesson in true penitence, carried a bitter-gourd with him, and
whenever the Namboodiri took a ritual bath in a sacred pond
or river to wash off his sin, Chathan washed the gourd too.

When they returned home, Chathan diced the gourd and
gave it to the Namboodiri's wife for cooking, and she, not
suspecting it to be bitter, prepared a curry with it and served
it to her husband for lunch along with rice and other dishes.
Predictably, the Namboodiri choked on tasting the bitter
curry and rebuked his wife for her carelessness in cooking.
But she pleaded innocence, and put the blame on Chathan
for giving her the bitter-gourd.

When questioned, Chathan feigned surprise that the gourd
was bitter. 'I had washed it in all the sacred waters where
you had bathed,' he said. 'How can it still be bitter?'

'Will the gourd lose its bitterness even if you wash it in
Ganga water!' mocked the Namboodiri.

'Well, if the gourd is bitter even after all those ritual
washings,' submitted Chathan, 'I doubt whether you have
really washed off your sin.'

The Namboodiri was taken aback by Chathan's insolent
retort, but he soon realized that Chathan was indeed right,
and asked him what he should do to clear his conscience.

'You should make a metal statue of the woman you were
infatuated with, heat it red-hot, and embrace it before a
gathering of people after confessing your sin to them,' advised
Chathan. 'That is the only remedy.'

The simple-minded Namboodiri then had a statue of the

woman made, and invited the public to witness his rite of atonement. Then, placing the heated statue before them, he confessed his sin, and turned to embrace the statue.

Just then Chathan intervened to stop him.

'Enough! Your sins are forgiven,' Chathan said, and went on to explain that it was sincere repentance that earns forgiveness of sin, not rites and pilgrimages.

Later, Chathan taught his master yet another lesson, this time in true piety. The Namboodiri was in the habit of taking a pre-dawn ritual bath every day and spending several hours in devotions. Chathan was curious about this, and one day asked him what he did the whole morning.

'I worship Para-brahma,' replied the Namboodiri loftily.

'What is Para-brahma like?' asked Chathan.

'Like a buffalo,' joked the Namboodiri.

But Chathan took him seriously, and from that day on he too followed the Namboodiri's practice of religiously worshipping Para-brahma, visualizing the god as a buffalo. As a result, after forty days of devotions, Para-brahma appeared before him in the form of a buffalo, and thereafter began to follow him about, though invisible to others.

The Namboodiri did not know any of this, and had no reason to suspect that god had appeared before Chathan after just a few weeks of devotions, when he himself had not had that privilege even after many years of devotions. But he realized the error of his ways one day when he and Chathan, with the invisible buffalo in tow, were going to a neighbouring village. On the way they had to pass through a narrow gate, which the buffalo was not able to cross because of the spread of its horns.

'Turn your head sideways and enter,' Chathan told the buffalo.

Hearing this, the Namboodiri, who was walking head, turned and asked: 'Who are you talking to?'

'To the buffalo,' said Chathan.

'Buffalo? Where?'

'There, don't you see? It's the Para-brahma that appeared to me when I worshipped him according to your advice,' said Chathan.

'I don't see anything,' said the Namboodiri.

'Touch me and look again,' said Chathan.

When the Namboodiri did so, he saw the buffalo. And it then dawned on him that it was true devotion, not idols and rituals, that was required for god-realization.

Arakkal Bibi

Kerala, a narrow sliver of land at the southern tip of the Indian subcontinent and far away from the path of invaders, has never been, unlike the rest of India, ruled by Muslim conquerors, although the sultans of Mysore did make a couple of brief forays into the region in the latter half of the eighteenth century. There were, however, many Muslim settlements in Kerala right from the beginning of the history of Islam, Arab traders who lived in amicable relationship with the local people. There was even a family of Muslim chieftains who ruled over a small principality in Malabar for many centuries from around the twelfth century. Their rule, however, was not established by conquest; it arose out of the normal social processes of Kerala, and was typical of the peculiarly harmonious social ethos of the region, despite its bewildering multiplicity of castes, creeds and communities.

Our story concerns a princess of the Kolathiri royal family that ruled over one of the many tiny kingdoms into which Kerala was divided in medieval times. The seat of the raja was at Ezhimala, a few kilometres to the north of Kannur, where he lived in a fortified palace on a river bank at the foot of the mountains, close to the sea. The fort had a flight of steps leading to the river, for the members of the royal family to go down to bathe.

One day, so goes the legend, when the princess was sporting in the river along with her younger sister, she was caught in the rapids and began to flounder, though her sister managed to swim ashore. Fortunately a Muslim youth who was passing by heard the cries of the princess, and he immediately plunged into the river to rescue her. Reaching her, he seized her by her hand and with some difficulty brought her to safety. But she shrank from rising out of the water. Realizing that this was because her clothes had got washed away in the river, the youth removed the shoulder-cloth that he had tied around his waist when he leapt into the river and gave it to her. He then discreetly withdrew from there.

The princess then wrapped the cloth—it was a new, unwashed length of cotton—around her waist and returned to the fort with her sister. She however refused to enter the palace, but remained in an outhouse. When her mother asked her why she was behaving so strangely, she said, 'That Muslim youth had taken my hand and had given me a new dhoti to wear.'

'What're you saying, my child?' her mother asked in consternation, realizing that what the princess had described was an act of the customary marriage practice of her community.

'Yes, by taking his hand and accepting the cloth he offered, I have become his wife,' said the princess. 'But since it is not proper for a princess to marry a Muslim, I'm now an outcaste. I cannot enter the palace.'

Hearing of this, her uncle, the raja, decided to perform the necessary purificatory rituals to enable her to return to the family fold. But the princess refused to go through the rites. In the end the raja, in consultation with the senior members of his family, decided to give her in marriage to the Muslim youth.

She then became a Muslim, and it was according to Muslim rites that her marriage was performed. The raja endowed her richly and built for her a separate palace nearby, so that, as an heiress under the matrilineal system followed by the royal family, her status would not be in any way inferior to that of the other princesses, despite her unconventional marriage. The youth, who was a common soldier in the raja's army, was promoted to a high rank and provided with a suitable retinue.

After her marriage, the princess came to be known as Arakkal Bibi, which was her Muslim title, and her family adopted a blend of Hindu and Muslim customs. She did observe purdah, but not as strictly as women in other Muslim noble families, so that her relatives and other local princes could visit her freely. And her family observed the matrilineal system as among Nairs.

Around this time, a minister of the kingdom, Arayankulangara Nair, also became a convert to Islam, and took the name Muhammad Ali, and he later married, with royal consent, a princess of the Arakkal family. Ali's descendants also served the raja, and one of them, Ali Moossa, became renowned for his naval exploit that brought the Lakshadweep Islands under Kolathiri rule. For that feat, the raja rewarded Ali with extensive fiefs and conferred on him the title Azhi Raja (King of the Ocean), which in time became corrupted as Ali Raja. The Kolathiri raja also assigned the Kannur fort to Ali Moossa, and he, along with the Arakkal family, took up his residence there.

Towards the end of the eighteenth century, the fiefdom

became a virtually independent principality, but was soon after absorbed into the Madras Presidency when the East India Company conquered Malabar. The British pensioned off the Muslim chieftain.

∾

POT LUCK

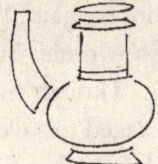

Darkness, as the saying goes, is never more intense than just before the first light of dawn. That at any rate was the experience of Pandaparambath Bhattathiri, an impoverished Brahmin living in a small, dilapidated house in a coastal village in north Kerala. The family was so destitute that they were barely able to stave off starvation. But their fortune turned entirely in just one day. That day, while Bhattathiri was sitting dejected and hungry in the veranda of his cottage in the evening, waiting for his wife to serve him the rice gruel she was preparing, he saw a man landing a boat on the beach close to his house. This, it turned out, was a shipwrecked Chinese merchant, and he, seeing Bhattathiri, went up to him and told him his tale of woe, of how he lost all his men and possessions in a storm.

'I've lost everything in the storm,' said the merchant. 'I haven't even had anything to eat or drink since yesterday.'

Hearing the merchant's story and overcome with pity for his plight, Bhattathiri, though famished himself, went into the kitchen and brought out the pot of rice gruel that his wife had prepared.

'This is all the food we have at home,' said Bhattathiri, serving the gruel to the merchant. 'We ourselves are in dire straits.'

The merchant ate that humble meal with great relish. 'What you've given me is not just food, but my very life,' he said. 'All my life I'll cherish the flavour of this gruel. And if fate brings me to these shores again, I'll reward you suitably for the kindness you've shown me. But now I've to seek yet another favour from you. Though most of my goods were lost in the storm, I've managed to save a few jars, and these I would like to leave here for safekeeping.'

Bhattathiri was reluctant to accept the responsibility. 'This house is too small and dilapidated, and it's not safe to keep anything valuable here,' he protested.

'There's nothing very valuable in the jars,' assured the merchant. 'Only dried lentil.'

'In that case I've no objection,' said Bhattathiri.

The merchant then deposited ten sealed jars in the house and departed, and Bhattathiri gave no further thought to the matter. But a few days later, when his children were howling with hunger, his wife suggested that they should take some lentil from one of the jars to feed the children. Bhattathiri rejected the suggestion, saying, 'How can we take for ourselves what has been entrusted to us for safekeeping? It's better to die than break trust.'

'It'll be no sin if we take some lentil to save the lives of our little children,' persisted the woman. 'In any case, by the time the merchant returns we can somehow fill the jar again. Even if we can't, he'll surely forgive us. After all, he himself has known the pangs of hunger.'

In the end Bhattathiri yielded to her plea. But when he opened one of the jars and scooped out some lentil into a vessel, he heard a metallic tinkle and, on examining the contents of the jar with a lamp, found that it was filled with gold coins, with only a layer of lentil on top. The other jars too, he found, were filled with gold coins. He did not say anything about this to his wife, but took one coin from a jar and carefully re-sealed all the jars. Then he went to the market and bought provisions with the coin, and for the first time after many years the family was able to eat to their heart's content for several days.

Meanwhile the gold coins in the jars began to work on Bhattathiri's mind. 'I've anyhow broken trust by opening the jars, so I might as well go ahead and use the gold in them to make my fortune,' he reasoned. 'It may take the merchant several years to return, and by then I might be able to fill the jars with gold again.' Though his conscience still troubled him, in the end necessity won over conscience, and Bhattathiri began to regularly dip into the jars, to invest the money in paddy fields and coconut groves, and to build a mansion for himself. Gradually he acquired a large estate, and by the prudent management of his affairs, came to have a net saving of over twelve thousand rupees a year. With this saving he bought gold coins, and within a few years was able to fill all the merchant's jars again with gold. Then he bought another ten jars, half the size of the other jars, and filled these too with gold coins.

After some twelve years, the Chinese merchant returned. When he saw the transformation of the house where he had deposited his jars, he felt certain that Bhattathiri had appropriated the gold and that he had no chance of getting it back. But he thought that he should at least ask Bhattathiri about it.

Bhattathiri received the merchant with courtesy and, after

customary salutations, confessed that he had indeed used the merchant's gold for some transactions. 'I beg your forgiveness for doing that. I'll now return all your gold with interest.'

Bhattathiri then brought out the ten jars of the merchant as well as his own ten small jars, and placed them before the merchant. 'These small jars contain gold coins to cover the interest on the gold I've taken from you,' he said.

The merchant, relieved that he was getting his money back, refused to accept the small jars. 'I should be paying you a fee for keeping my gold safe instead of taking interest from you,' he protested.

'All the wealth that I've gained is by investing your gold, so it's only proper that I should pay you interest,' said Bhattathiri.

Again the merchant refused the offer. 'I've suffered no loss from leaving the gold here,' he said. 'If you have gained by it, it's only because of your enterprise and good fortune. Besides, if I take anything that is not rightfully mine, fortune will desert me.'

Thus pressed, Bhattathiri reluctantly took back the small jars. The merchant then ceremonially—by offering an oblation of water, flowers and betel leaves, as was customary in Kerala—presented Bhattathiri one of his own gold-filled jars as a token of his appreciation of the man's integrity.

Now it so happened that the mouth of this jar was slightly out of shape, but the merchant said: 'Though a little deformed, this is a very lucky jar. There will never be want in the house where it is kept.'

And so it was. Bhattathiri's family kept the jar for several generations and continued to prosper.

Royal Pranks

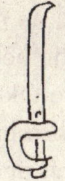

In fourteenth century Kerala, when the Zamorins of Kozhikode ruled over most of Malabar, the region immediately to the north of their kingdom was ruled by Kolathiri rajas. The two kings maintained an overtly amicable relationship, and often visited each other, but there was an undercurrent of rivalry between them, as was common among neighbouring kings. This sometimes led to war, and at other times to a battle of wits.

Our story concerns the pranks the two rajas played on each other following a bantering exchange between them during a visit of the Kolathiri raja to Kozhikode. The Zamorin showed his royal guest all the courtesies expected of him, but their repartees also had a cutting edge to them.

'Will S*amoori* gore?' asked the Kolathiri raja in jest one evening, using the shortened form of the title of the Kozhikode ruler and emphasizing its last two syllables to mean 'bull'.

The Zamorin chuckled over this witticism and countered it with a quip of his own. 'Will Kola*thiri* burn?' he asked, playing on the word *thiri* to mean 'wick'.

'Yes,' said the other. 'Kolathiri might burn. Be careful.'

'If Kolathiri burns, Samoori will gore,' retorted the Zamorin.

A few months after the Kolathiri raja returned to his capital, he sent to the Zamorin an intricately carved wooden box as a present. The box had a secret chamber of gunpowder in it, and was so constructed as to burst into flames when opened, to prove that Kolathiri would indeed burn.

The Zamorin suspected as much. Therefore when the messenger presented him the box, he gave it to one of his attendants and asked him to take it to a pond and immerse it in water for a while and then bring it back. Because of this precaution, when the box was opened, the gunpowder, being sodden, did not burn. The crestfallen Kolathiri envoy then returned home and informed his king that the trick had failed.

Then it was the turn of the Zamorin to retaliate. And he now sent an envoy to the Kolathiri raja, bearing, as a present, an ornamental box similar to the one he had received. 'This must be a trick like the one I tried to play on him,' thought the raja, and sent the box to be immersed in water. When it was brought back, the raja took out its key and opened it with a knowing chuckle. But instead of gunpowder the box was packed with the nests of hornets, and as the box opened, the hornets, maddened by the dunking, swarmed over the raja and stung him severely. He had forgotten that the Zamorin was expected to gore or sting, not burn.

As a political and military strategist too the Zamorin proved himself to be the craftier of the two rajas, and in the course of time he brought the Kolathiri kingdom under his sphere of influence, though the Kolathiri royal family itself endured into modern times and played an important role in the tussle between various Kerala rulers and European powers.

A Kathakali Legend

Kathakali, the unique dance form of Kerala, though commonly described as classical dance, is of relatively recent origin, having evolved only in the seventeenth century from the older Krishnattam and Ramanattam dance-drama traditions, which in turn had evolved from the many centuries older ritual theatre called Kudiyattam. Even after Kathakali emerged as a distinct dance form, it underwent major changes over the years. In the early days, the costume and make-up of the different types of Kathakali characters were not as elaborate and stylized as they would be in later times, and the performers themselves used to sing the lyrics. The introduction of musicians to sing the lyrics, the use of mask-like facial make-up, and the adoption of intricate hand gestures and facial expressions, are all innovations attributed to Kaplingat Namboodiri, a renowned Kathakali singer and impresario.

Namboodiris in medieval Kerala were usually patrons of the performing arts, not themselves performers, and there is a legend about how Kaplingat came to be a performer. His ancestral home was in Cheruthuruthi, a small town about twenty-five kilometres north of Thrissur, where poet Vallathol would later, in the mid-twentieth century, establish the famous dance institute, Kerala Kalamandalam. When Kaplingat's mother was pregnant with him, her husband, it is said, sought the blessing of a saint living at the local temple to make the childbirth auspicious. Hearing of it, the temple priest also made a similar request for his pregnant Varier wife.

The saint acceded to the requests, and every day for forty days he handed over to the priest two small packets of butter sanctified with mantras, indicating which was for whom. Now the priest, thinking that there was something special in the butter given for the Namboodiri's wife, transposed the packets, and gave to his own wife what was meant for the Namboodiri's wife.

In due course both women gave birth to boys, but it so happened that though the Namboodiri couple were handsome and fair complexioned, their child was not at all like them, while the priest and his wife, though themselves dark and unprepossessing, were blessed with a child of exceptional radiance. This was attributed to the transposed butter packets. And as the children grew up, the Varier boy showed Brahminical aptitudes in being diligent in ritual practices and in learning the scriptures, while the Namboodiri boy (Kaplingat) was indifferent to such matters but was keen on the Varier vocations of singing, drumming and carpentry. In time, the Varier boy became a distinguished scholar, while Kaplingat became a renowned Kathakali exponent, with his own troupe, in which he was himself the star singer.

Kaplingat, like most creative people, was a non-conformist, and remained so even at the height of his fame, and there are several legends about his oddities. It is said that once, when he was at the house of Poomulli Namboodiri to give a performance, and the two Namboodiris were at their evening bath and devotions, he stood facing the east, instead of the west as required.

'That's the east, not the west,' Poomulli told him. 'You've to turn around.'

'I know I'm facing the east,' said Kaplingat. 'But I've to first perform the morning rite before turning to the west for the evening rite.'

'You haven't performed the morning rite!'

'Where was the time? I had no time even to have a bath till now,' said Kaplingat.

'What happened?'

His drumhead, said Kaplingat, had broken the previous night during a performance, so early morning he had to go to a nearby village to get a piece of leather from a Parayan who usually had hides in his hut for sale. But when he got there, the Parayan was not at home, nor were there any hides in his hut. Fortunately, on the way back he found an abandoned old cow on the wayside.

'I tied up the cow and skinned it to make the drumhead,' said Kaplingat.

'Enough! Enough!' cried Poomulli, stopping his ears with his hands. 'I don't want to hear anything more. Cow slaughter! Shiva-shiva!'

'Anyway, that's why I could not perform my morning rite,' went on Kaplingat. 'But even if late, I perform all the daily rites.' He then asked for a lamp, some flowers and sandalwood paste, to perform the Salagramam puja.

'Won't you need Salagramam also?' asked Poomulli. Salagramam—a coiled, striated fossil shell, worshipped by Brahmins as an emblem of Vishnu—was essential for the puja.

'No,' said Kaplingat. 'I always carry Salagramam with me.'

'Really?' Poomulli was surprised. 'Where is it?'

'Well, since it's a nuisance to carry about the whole Salagramam, I have broken off a piece from it and put it on the ring I wear,' said Kaplingat.

Poomulli was outraged. 'You broke Salagramam? Shiva-shiva! What a sin!' he exclaimed and walked away in disgust. And Kaplingat, who had not slept a wink the previous night, went to lie down for a while and get some sleep, telling his troupe to begin the performance at the usual time, and that he would join them later.

He slept through a good part of the performance, and this angered Poomulli, for the main attraction of Kaplingat's troupe was his own singing. Piqued, he went in to wake up Kaplingat. But when he pushed open the door of the room where Kaplingat was sleeping, he found him lying there enveloped in a blinding supernatural radiance, in the form of Lord Vishnu himself. Shocked into the recognition of the divine nature of the artist, Poomulli prostrated silently before him and quietly withdrew.

Halfway through the performance Kaplingat woke up and came to the stage. And his singing that night, it is said, was truly divine.

❧

Divine Madness

One of the most celebrated folklore personages of Kerala was a Sisyphean character known as Naranath Bhrandhan, the Madman of Naranam. It was his practice to spend several hours every day laboriously rolling up a large boulder to the top of a bald hillock near his village, and then let it roll down free as he stood at the crest of the hill clapping his hands and roaring with insane laughter. But unlike Sisyphus, whose endless, unavailing toil was a punishment exacted by gods, Bhrandhan's was a labour of love.

Why did he do it? Bhrandhan's only answer to the query was to laugh heartily. In time, however, people came to interpret his act as a metaphor of the human predicament, the transience of fortune and the ultimate futility of human endeavours. Bhrandhan thus came to be revered as one touched by some mysterious divine grace.

Bhrandhan would rise with the sun every day and labour till noon rolling the stone. After this, he would set out to seek alms, carrying a copper cooking vessel under his arm. Wherever he found himself in the evening, there he would build a fire, cook the rice he had got as alms, and eat his only meal of the day. Then he would stretch himself out on the ground there and sleep.

Now it so happened that one winter night Bhrandhan found himself in a cemetery after his round of begging. A corpse had been cremated there that evening and the cinders were still glowing. That suited Bhrandhan, and he set up a fireplace there with the stones lying around, collected some twigs and built a fire using the embers of the funeral pyre. Then he brought water for cooking from a nearby stream, and set the rice to cook. He sat close by, humming tunelessly and warming himself, favouring his left leg, which was infected with elephantiasis.

In a while, as the rice slowly cooked, Bhrandhan dozed off. Soon it was midnight. And presently, as the witching hour turned, Chutala Bhadrakali—Kali of the cremation ground—arrived there with a host of howling nether-world spirits, all leaping and stomping, to perform their ritual dance on the funeral pyre. But they stopped short on seeing Bhrandhan, amazed to find anyone at all in the cremation ground at that hour, more so one who paid no attention to their terrifying presence.

'Who are you?' Kali challenged.

'A man,' returned Bhrandhan. 'Don't you have eyes to see?'

'Begone!' she ordered.

'Begone? Why should I?' asked Bhrandhan. 'I won't.'

'You won't!' Kali was astounded. 'Do you know who I am?'

'I don't know,' said Bhrandhan, 'and I don't care.'

'I'm Bhadrakali,' she said. 'We'll scare you off if you don't leave.'

Bhrandhan was amused. 'All right,' he said. 'Scare me then.'

So they rushed at him from all sides, shrieking and

howling, rolling bloodshot eyes and baring tigerish canines. But that only made Bhrandhan laugh. It then dawned on Kali that this was no ordinary man that she was dealing with.

'Done?' Bhrandhan asked. 'Are you done with scaring me?'

Abashed, she then pleaded with him to move away, so they could perform their funeral dance.

'Go ahead and dance,' said Bhrandhan. 'Why should I leave for that?'

'It's not our custom to dance in the presence of men,' she said.

'Then do it tomorrow,' said Bhrandhan. 'Whatever you say, I won't leave now.'

'The rite has to be performed today,' she persisted. 'That's our custom.'

'Well, I've my own custom too—to eat where I cook, and sleep where I eat,' said Bhrandhan. 'I won't leave.'

They wrangled about this for a while, but in the end it was Kali who had to back off. 'We will go then,' she said. 'But there is one other matter—whenever we run into men we cannot leave without either cursing them or granting them a boon. Please choose a boon.'

'I don't want any boon,' said Bhrandhan. 'Just leave. The rice is cooked and I want to eat.'

'Please don't say that,' she beseeched. 'We can't go without blessing you.'

'What a nuisance!' Bhrandhan groused. 'All right, can you tell me when I will die?'

'Certainly,' she said. 'You'll die in exactly thirty-six years, six months, twelve days, five hours and three minutes from this moment.'

'I would like to live one more day than that,' said

Bhrandhan. 'You can grant me that boon.'

'I'm sorry,' she said. 'I've no power to extend your life even by a minute.'

'All right then, let me die a day before the allotted time.'

'I can't reduce your lifespan either,' she confessed.

'I knew it!' he laughed. 'You have no power.'

'I have,' she said. 'But please ask for something that is in my power to grant.'

'Can you at least transfer the elephantiasis from my left leg to the right leg?' he asked.

'Of course,' she said, relieved, and granted him the boon and vanished.

Instantly, his right leg swelled up while the left leg returned to its normal shape. Bhrandhan then shifted position to keep his right leg close to the fire. In a while he ate his meal, and, contented, curled up on the ground close to the warmth of the funeral pyre and slept.

No Pain, No Gain

Many centuries ago, when spice trade ruled the oceans, Kozhikode in north Kerala was a world-renowned emporium, and its raja, the Zamorin, enjoyed considerable power and prestige. All those glories are now long gone. Though the head of the old ruling family still bears the royal title, he no longer enjoys any princely privileges. In fact, a raja in recent times even had to earn his living as a humble schoolteacher. And Kozhikode itself has lost much of its prominence. However, Lakshmi, the goddess of wealth, has not altogether abandoned the town, and her presence there is believed to be indicated by a peculiar lustre over its main bazaar in the evenings.

There is a legend behind this belief.

The story is that a Zamorin of the early nineteenth century was once afflicted with a mysterious ailment, a persistent sharp pain in his right shoulder. Though several physicians, occultists and astrologers tried their hand at treating the raja, the medicines and penances they prescribed had no effect whatever. The ailment seemed incurable.

At this juncture there arrived at the court an itinerant

wizard who, on being told about the raja's affliction, offered
to cure him. 'No elaborate treatment is required for this,' he
said confidently. 'All you have to do is to place a wet towel
on the shoulder, and the pain will cease immediately.'

No one believed him. But the raja, nearly driven out of
his mind by the excruciating pain, was willing to try anything,
however absurd it seemed. Miraculously, the simple remedy
worked. As soon as the wet towel was placed on the ailing
shoulder, the pain ceased. Delighted with the miraculous cure,
the raja honoured the wizard with a hero-bracelet and heaped
on him rich rewards. And the wizard went on his way.

When all this happened, the diwan, the wisest man in the
Zamorin's service, was not in the palace, but was attending
to some personal work at home, so he came to hear of the
cure only later in the day. The news appalled him, for he had
known all along the reason for the raja's illness and the means
to relieve him, but had deliberately refrained from acting on
it. 'What a misfortune!' he exclaimed, and hurriedly left
home. Afterwards he was seen rushing about in Kozhikode,
as if distractedly searching for someone. By evening he arrived
at the main bazaar of the town. And there, at a street corner,
he at last found the person he was looking for, a young
woman of luminous beauty.

'Lucky that I've run into you here,' he said to her. 'I've
something most important to tell you.'

The woman was curious. 'What's it? Tell me,' she said.

The diwan then fumbled in the tuck of his dhoti, as though
to take out something, and, seemingly distressed at not
finding it, said, 'God! I've left behind my official seal. I've to
dash back and get it. But I'll be back in a moment. Could
you please wait for me?'

'Alright,' she said.

'It's not enough that you just say it,' urged the diwan. 'I would like you to take an oath on it, for what I have to tell you is so very important.'

She agreed and swore that she would wait there till he returned. The diwan then hastened to the royal palace, and, appearing before the raja, said, 'I hear that you have been cured of your shoulder pain.'

'Yes, indeed,' said the raja. 'That wizard has truly amazing powers.'

'No doubt,' responded the diwan. 'But it was a terrible blunder to follow his advice without properly thinking about it or even consulting me. However, what is done is done. There's no point in crying over it. I knew what was ailing you, and if you too had known that, you would not have taken this cure.'

'What do you mean?'

'Our land has so far enjoyed great prosperity during your reign. This was because goddess Lakshmi had taken residence in you,' said the diwan. 'The pain you felt was because Lakshmi was dancing on your right shoulder. Nothing is more offensive to her than placing a wet towel on one's right shoulder. The moment this is done, Lakshmi will depart, and her elder sister Alakshmi, the goddess of misfortune, will take her place. That spells ruin. The wizard knew this, and that was why he was able to cure you. But he did not care about its other consequences.'

'Shiva-shiva!' exclaimed the raja. 'What shall we do now?'

'Well, though Lakshmi has left the palace, she has not left the town,' said the diwan. 'I've contrived to keep her here by a stratagem.'

He then told the raja about seeing Lakshmi in the main bazaar—the beautiful woman he met there—and asking her to remain there till he returned.

'But what'll happen when you return?'

'I won't return.'

'How can you break your word given to the goddess?'

'I've to keep it only if I'm alive,' said the diwan mysteriously.

He immediately left the palace and, returning home, committed ritual suicide. Consequently, Lakshmi could not ever leave the bazaar, and it is her presence there that is said to endow the place with its evening radiance.

The story really is a parable, and its moral is that a life of ease is not conducive to gain. No pain, no gain. But the raja learned the lesson too late for his own good. In a few decades the dynasty lost its sceptre to the British. And Kozhikode declined, becoming a mere provincial town.

Sanku, Beloved Elephant

The people of Kerala have always had, for some odd reason, a quaint fondness for elephants, and elephant lore is the subject of many popular Kerala legends. The incongruity of gentleness in these seemingly fearsome behemoths evidently touches some emotional chord in them, and they look on elephants as intelligent, affectionate creatures, beasts only in form but otherwise almost human. Elephants were seldom used in battle in Kerala, but mainly to lead temple processions, and this too fostered in people a devotional attitude towards them.

One of the most renowned temple elephants of Kerala was Thiruneelakhandan—affectionately called Sanku—owned by the Vaikam temple in central Kerala in the nineteenth century. There are no heroic deeds associated with this elephant, but he was highly esteemed for his intelligence and equable temperament, and it was said of him that he was a Brahmin among elephants. He had a proud bearing, and though there were often other elephants bigger than Sanku in temple processions, such was the way he carried himself that he was invariably given the privilege of carrying the idol.

He had a fine sense of music too, and was known to flap his ears in tune with the processional music.

Sanku's chief mahout throughout his adult life was Govindan Nair, who treated him as if he were his own child. On waking up in the morning, his first thought was always about Sanku, and he would not even take a sip of water without first feeding the elephant. And Sanku in turn showed true filial affection for Govindan, and would respond to his call even when standing far away, trumpeting loudly and running to him, like an obedient and affectionate child. Govindan never had any occasion to beat Sanku or even scold him, for the elephant always obeyed his soft-spoken directions.

Sanku was so good-natured that he was seldom kept chained, even at night. He never wandered away to forage, but would always stand in his allotted place, eat the fodder given to him, and then lie down there and sleep. Whenever there was a feast in the temple (which was nearly every other day in Vaikam) a huge vessel of rice and payasam (a sweetened rice and milk preparation) would be set aside for Sanku, and as soon as he saw the priests and other functionaries come out of the temple dining hall after their meal, he would, without anyone calling him, go to the entrance of the hall and stand there to be fed. Govindan or someone else would then make the rice into large balls and feed him. After eating his fill, he would return to his usual place, but he would not leave until he was fed, or if the quantity given to him was less than the usual amount.

Anyone could adorn him and lead him out for procession. But he was particular that only Govindan and the man carrying the idol should mount him from the front; all others had to mount from the back. He was familiar with the temple procession routine, knew where to stand and for how long, where to go, when to walk fast, when to walk slowly, and so on, so that he could be taken for processions even without a mahout in attendance.

Unlike some elephants, Sanku was never jealous of the presence of other elephants in the procession, and had never gored any. But he was not timid, and he knew how to deal with truculent elephants. Once an envious elephant, seeing Sanku heading a procession, advanced on him threateningly, its tail held high and ears outstretched tensely. As the elephant charged, pandemonium broke out among the vast assembled crowd, and everyone ran helter-skelter, but Sanku stood his ground. He took with his trunk the long mahout's stick that Govindan gave him and, as the other elephant drew near, gave him a sharp blow with it. Immediately the elephant turned tail and fled, crying loudly, and went and hid himself somewhere far away, shivering. And Sanku continued with the procession, as if nothing unusual had happened.

He had never hurt any of his mahouts, except once accidentally knocking down Govindan during a procession. The moment he saw Govindan fall, he stopped, and none of the other mahouts could make him move on. He stood there, making thin, piping noises of contrition, and resumed the procession only after Govindan regained consciousness and spoke to him. People then carried Govindan to his house. As soon as the procession ended, Sanku rushed to Govindan's house and remained there for the rest of the day, and thereafter took to going and standing in the front yard of the house every day till Govindan recovered fully and began to move about.

Sanku was usually not sent outside Travancore for any work, but once, on the special request of the raja of Kochi, he was taken there to lead a temple procession. That proved unlucky, for he fell seriously ill on returning—because someone had cast an evil eye on him, it was said—and it was only after a long treatment that he recovered. But he never fully regained his strength, and seemed to waste away. Towards the end, he was not even able to swallow the plantains placed in his mouth. As Sanku lay dying, Govindan remained with him day and night till the very end, often shedding tears, while the elephant now and then caressed him consolingly with his trunk. In popular view, there has never been, and there will never be, an elephant and a mahout like Sanku and Govindan.

The Veda of Life

A good physician, according to *Charaka Samhita*, an ancient Indian medical classic, should have four essential qualities—thorough knowledge, extensive experience, resourcefulness, and cleanliness. Vayaskara Narayanan Moossad, the legendary nineteenth century physician of Kerala and son of the equally renowned Achan Moossad, had all these qualities, and was in addition blessed with rugged common sense, so he could boldly modify textual prescriptions to treat seemingly incurable diseases.

Narayanan was a child prodigy. He began his medical practice at the age of sixteen, having by then mastered all the scriptures and Ayurvedic texts. Despite his young age, he was invariably successful in his treatments, and in a short time earned a reputation rivalling that of his father.

Characteristic of Narayanan's innovative approach was the treatment he prescribed for Sankunni Moossad, an ailing relative. A small boil, about the size of a grain of rice, had once formed on the back of Sankunni's neck. He did not pay any attention to it, and one morning when he was having a haircut, the boil got nipped off. It did not hurt then, but by evening, the abscess swelled to the size of an eggplant and became very painful. Sankunni, being a physician himself— he was the personal physician of the Zamorin of Kozhikode— tried all the known cures, but found no relief. In a few days the abscess grew to the size of a small coconut and the inflammation began to spread to his face. The pain was now so excruciating that he was not able to eat anything or sleep. In that predicament he decided to consult Narayanan Moossad, even though that involved some loss of face for himself as a physician. A messenger was then sent to Vayaskara with a letter.

Narayanan set out within an hour of getting the letter. But it took him three days to reach Sankunni's village, as the two families lived at a great distance from each other, in different parts of Kerala, and he had to travel by rowboat and cart, as there was no motor transport those days. Meanwhile, several other senior physicians had tried their hand at treating Sankunni, but with little effect. As soon as Narayanan got there, he took a bath and went to see the patient. He found Sankunni reclining with his face down against a rolled-up mattress, with tears streaming down his cheeks, unable even to speak. The attending physicians told Narayanan that Sankunni had got to that state of exhaustion because he had not eaten anything for several days. He had a longing to drink milk, but physicians advised him against it, as milk was contraindicated for the treatment of his condition.

Narayanan overruled them, saying that there was no harm in giving milk. He then had a tumbler of hot milk brought to him, sweetened it with plenty of sugar, and slowly trickled it into the parched mouth of the patient with a spoon made of a leaf of the jackfruit tree. Sankunni sipped slowly and painfully, but was able to drink all the milk in about an hour.

'I feel better now,' Sankunni told Narayanan after drinking the milk and resting for a while. 'You can decide on my treatment later, but first go and have your meal. You must be tired after the long journey.'

Later that day Narayanan Moossad examined the patient thoroughly and decided on the mode of treatment. To the surprise of other physicians, his main prescription consisted of milk mixed with various herbs, which was given to the patient two or three times a day for a few days. That restored the patient's strength somewhat. Moossad then prepared a herbal paste and applied it to the abscess. In a few days the abscess came to a head and burst, draining all the pus. Then another paste was applied to heal the wound. All this took several weeks, and during this entire period Narayanan stayed with the patient, to ensure his full recovery.

'So you can cure even incurable diseases!' a local physician one day said to Narayanan by way of complimenting him.

'It's said that any disease can be cured if treated skilfully, and the physician has the healing touch,' Narayanan said modestly. 'That's all there is to it.'

'But where is it said that you can give milk to a patient suffering from this disease? I have not found it in any of my books.'

'It's not in the books, but I decided to give milk because that was the only food the patient was able to take. And it was essential that he should take food, to sustain life and to gain strength to fight the disease,' Narayanan said. 'Ayurveda is the Veda of life. Our priority should be to do whatever is necessary to sustain life. As my father used to say, there's no treatment for the dead.'

While Narayanan was living with Sankunni and treating him, a messenger arrived there to summon Sankunni to the royal palace to treat the Zamorin who, curiously, was also suffering from a huge boil on his back. Sankunni, being unable to go himself, deputed Narayanan to attend on the raja.

Narayanan was received with some derision at the royal palace, because of his young age. But he ignored the muttered comments of the courtiers, quickly had a bath and went to examine the raja. Just then an official asked him to have his meal first. 'I've come here to treat the raja, not to have a feast,' Narayanan said curtly. 'I'll eat later.' After examining the raja, he picked a few green leaves from the palace compound and asked a palace servant to grind it in water and prepare a lotion. When this was applied to the boil, it burst and a good amount of blood and pus oozed out of it, giving immediate relief from pain to the raja. The raja was then given a bowl of rice gruel to eat, and was asked to rest for some time.

In a while the raja slept, and when he woke up after about four hours, he felt completely cured. The lesion had only to heal now, and Narayanan prescribed certain medicines for that. He then left for home, though the raja desired him to stay on for some days. He also politely refused to accept the presents offered by the raja, saying that he was only the representative of Sankunni, and did not deserve anything himself.

A Test for Wives

The eleven sons of the renowned sage Vararuchi, born of his liaison with a low-caste woman and abandoned by him in Kerala on their birth, are all said to have instinctively known, when they grew up, who their real father was, though each of them was brought up in a different place and by foster parents of different castes. And all of them used to get together once a year in the house of Agnihotri, their Brahmin brother, for the anniversary rites of their departed father.

On these occasions it was customary for the brothers to eat a meal together, despite their caste differences. Agnihotri's wife was initially reluctant to violate social taboos and attend on men of lower castes, and though eventually, on being pressed by her husband, she agreed to serve food to the brothers, it was by shielding herself from their sight with a palm-leaf umbrella that she appeared before them.

'What's this?' asked Pakkanar, a low-caste brother, seeing the peculiar habit of the woman.

'It is the custom of our caste that a virtuous wife should not allow herself to be seen by strangers,' explained Agnihotri.

'How strange,' said Pakkanar. 'How can virtue be in just

holding an umbrella or putting on a veil? I don't think your women know the true meaning of wifely virtue.'

'What do you low-caste people know about these things?' scorned Agnihotri.

'Come to my hut, and I will show you how a virtuous wife behaves,' said Pakkanar.

They argued about this for a while, and finally decided to settle the matter by putting their wives to a test. Pakkanar then took Agnihotri to his hut. As soon as they got there, he called his wife to him and asked her how much paddy there was in the house.

'Five measures,' she said.

'Husk half of it and cook the rice and bring it,' he said.

She immediately did what she was told, without a murmur. But when she brought the cooked rice, Pakkanar asked her to throw it away. Again she obeyed him without the slightest hesitation. He then asked her to husk the remaining paddy and cook that also. But this time too, when she brought the cooked rice, he asked her to throw it away. And once again she obeyed without demur, even though that was all the food they had in their hut and she had not eaten the whole day.

The brothers then returned to Agnihotri's house. 'Get your wife to do what my wife did,' said Pakkanar. But when Agnihotri asked his wife to husk two measures of paddy and cook it, she raised an objection. 'There is rice in the house, so why should I husk paddy?' she asked. It took much persuasion to make her do what she was told, and it was with a sullen pout that she brought the cooked rice and pushed it before Agnihotri.

'Throw it away,' Agnihotri said to her.

'What?'

'Throw it away,' Agnihotri repeated.

'Are you crazy?' she bristled. 'It's a shame to waste the food, especially after I had taken all the trouble to husk the paddy and cook the rice.'

With great difficulty and after much argument Agnihotri finally managed to get her to throw away the rice. Then he told her to husk two more measures of paddy and cook it.

'You're really mad!' she screamed. 'Am I to dance to every tune you play?'

She then flounced back into the house, and however much Agnihotri tried to reason with her, she would not listen.

'What do you say now?' asked Pakkanar. 'Do you now understand that wifely virtue is not in caste practices but in devotion to the husband and doing without argument what he tells her to do?'

This is the story. And to it Kottarathil Sankunni, the compiler of the *Ithihyamala*, has attached a comment: 'Modern people might not all agree with the moral of this story. But it is not proper for a virtuous wife to squabble with her husband. If indeed he sometimes tells her to do something unreasonable, she should gently reason with him to change his mind, and not pick a fight with him. A quarrelsome wife is not a helpmate but a hell-mate.'

True indeed. But we should today add that the maintenance of marital harmony is as much the responsibility of the husband as of the wife. If a quarrelsome wife is a hell-mate, so is a quarrelsome husband.

❧

A Martial Joust

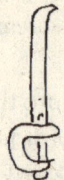

In medieval Kerala, fighting wars was a favourite pastime of chieftains, and martial jousts a popular spectator sport. These practices gradually died out in early modern times, but kalaris, martial arts gymnasiums, continued to flourish in a few places in Kerala well into the nineteenth century, and kalari champions remained very much the folk heroes.

One such hero was Kelu Menon of the Perumbulavil family in north Kerala. Kelu was by nature high-spirited and wilful, and even as a child he used to buck at the authority of the family elders. Eventually, when he was about sixteen years old, he ran away from home, to make his own way in the world. Fortunately, an affluent Nair family in southern Kerala took him in as a ward, and he lived with them for twelve years. It was during this period that he acquired his skill as a swordsman, learning the art from Changambally Gurukkal, a renowned Muslim martial arts exponent of the time.

At the age of twenty-eight Kelu, his wild spirit somewhat tamed, returned home. The family was pleased with the return of the prodigal son. They attributed his transformation to Gurukkal, and, wishing to honour and reward him, invited him home one day, making elaborate preparations to entertain him, especially minding the fact that he was a man of high standing in his community.

When Gurukkal arrived at the Perumbulavil house, it so happened that Kelu was not at home. Gurukkal took advantage of this to arrange for a spontaneous demonstration of the skill of his disciple, and had the trunk of a banana tree planted in the courtyard of the house with an iron rod inserted into it. When Kelu came and made his obeisance, Gurukkal asked him whether he could cut down the banana tree trunk with a single slash of his sword. Kelu rightly suspected that this was done to test his skill and that there would be some rod inserted into the trunk. So it was with a ferocious swipe that he struck the trunk, a blow so hard that his sword not only sliced through the trunk and the iron rod in it but also smashed a granite trough lying at its foot.

'Why did you use so much force?' Gurukkal scolded him.

'I thought there might be a copper rod inside, not an iron rod,' Kelu said apologetically.

'Good,' said Gurukkal. 'It's always prudent to overestimate the strength of the opponent rather than underestimate it.'

Because of his martial prowess, Kelu was in time appointed as the village headman. Even then he did not entirely give up his wild ways, and was once very nearly caught while raiding a rich merchant's house in Kunnamkulam near Thrissur, supposedly in the Robin Hood style of robbing the rich to help the poor. Gradually his reputation spread, and he became quite a folk hero.

However, despite the high status that he now enjoyed, Kelu's dress and appearance remained simple, and his bearing modest, so that strangers often did not realize what a dangerous man they were dealing with. Thus one day, when

Kelu was walking along a narrow embankment between paddy fields, he was confronted by an opulently dressed gent, who asked him insolently to step aside and let him pass. Kelu, though he was a man of violent temper, quietly stepped aside, but while the other man passed, he jabbed him lightly with a finger at a particular spot. At the touch of his finger the other man collapsed into the muddy field, for Kelu was an expert in immobilizing adversaries by jabbing at marmams, vital spots, of which there are reckoned to be 108 in the human body. Kelu then went on his way. Though people tried to help the fallen man to his feet, he was unable to move, and had to lie there in the mud till Kelu came that way again and released him with a jab of his finger at another spot.

But Kelu was best known for his swordsmanship, of which he once gave a memorable demonstration in a contest between two rival kalaris during a puberty festivity in a chieftain's house. One of the contending schools was that of Kelu's old guru, who entered the fray hoping to win honours with Kelu's help. Unfortunately, at the time of the contest Kelu had gone to a distant place. Initially the students of the two schools sparred with each other and performed various gymnastics, and Gurukkal tried to delay the main event as much as possible, hoping that Kelu would arrive in time to save his honour.

For the final test of skill, an oil lamp was suspended on a metal chain from a beam. The lamp was filled to the brim with oil and all the wicks in it were lit. Immediately below the lamp was placed a wooden bushel, the mouth of which was just wide enough to take the base of the lamp. What was required in the test was for the contestant to cut the chain with a single blow of the sword so that the lamp would fall into the bushel precisely, but without spilling a drop of oil or blowing out a wick.

This was the feat that Gurukkal had hoped that Kelu would perform. But as he did not arrive even till the last moment, Gurukkal was obliged to enter the arena himself. He again tried to delay the test by finding fault with the swords given to him, breaking or bending them out of shape by flexing them in peculiar ways. Kurup, the rival guru, saw through Gurukkal's gambit and challenged him either to go ahead with the test or step aside so he himself could perform the feat. Kelu, who had by then arrived on the scene and was standing silently in the crowd, now stepped forward. Seeing him, the relieved Gurukkal gave him the sword, declaring that there was no need for him to execute the stunt himself, and that even a disciple of his could do it. And Kelu won the contest with ease, saving his guru's honour.

The Exorcist

Exorcism was the psychotherapy of the medieval world, and, if we are to go by folklore, it was no less effective than the modern methods. Every kind of mental disorder, from eccentricity to insanity, was in those days attributed to possession by a spirit, so the exorcist was a professional very much in demand. But he was more a feared than respected man, even though his methods were, in Kerala at any rate, relatively simple, without any of the bizarre paraphernalia commonly associated with his profession.

The rite of exorcism was ordinarily held in a specially erected flower-decked temporary shed in the victim's house, or, alternatively, in a Devi temple. The possessed, usually a woman, would sit in a magical circle drawn with ash on the floor of the shed, and the exorcist, veiled in thick coils of incense smoke, would sit facing her, chanting occult incantations in a low voice and ringing a brass hand-bell. There would be, on the floor between them, a slender cane that the exorcist had infused with occult potency; this was the chief instrument of exorcism.

Normally the rite would last only a few hours, but

sometimes, if the incubus was obstinate, it would go on for several days. If successful, the rite would end with the woman rising in a hypnotic trance, heaving and tossing wildly, and flagellating herself with the exorcist's cane. Sometimes the exorcist himself would scourge her. In the end the exhausted 'spirit' would disclose his identity and depart, swearing not to bother the woman again.

Occasionally complications would arise in the exorcism rite because of interference by other occultists. Thus a rite of Thevalassery Damodaran Nambi, a prominent eighteenth century exorcist of Kerala, was once disrupted by Usaka Raother, another prominent exorcist. They belonged to two different communities—Nambi was a Hindu, Raother a Muslim—but their rivalry was purely professional. The confrontation between the two took place over treating a woman possessed by a Gandharvan, an amorous semi-divine spirit. When Raother, who was consulted first to treat the woman, proved unsuccessful, the family called in Nambi. This upset Raother, for he feared that if Nambi succeeded where he had failed, it would mean loss of face for him. So he set out to thwart Nambi's rite.

Nambi belonged to a family of hereditary exorcists, and had received rigorous training in his profession for several years. After completing his training, he spent a further three years in devotions while observing a vow of silence, and culminated it by worshipping Devi at the Chengannoor temple uninterruptedly for forty-one days, in order to integrate and intensify his occult powers. And he continued to spend long hours every day worshipping Devi in the seclusion of a cellar in his house.

All this endowed Nambi with extraordinary occult power. This however was not evident to strangers, for his appearance was simple and his demeanour mild. This misled Raother into believing that he could easily thwart Nambi.

In fact, Nambi did not evoke much confidence in the possessed woman's husband either. Nambi was aware of this, but he ignored it and calmly went about preparing for the rite, first drawing on the floor of the exorcism shed an image of Gandharvan with coloured powder, then an occult circle to seat the woman, and finally a lotus diagram for him to offer puja.

When everything was ready, he lighted an oil lamp and performed an elaborate puja. Then he brought the possessed woman out of the house and seated her in the circle prepared for her, and began the exorcism rite. By then a good number of people had gathered to watch the rite, and among them was Raother. The rite took a long time, and consisted of prayers, invocations and occult acts, and at the end of it Nambi took a handful of sanctified flowers and parched paddy, muttered a mantra over them, and threw them on the head of the woman.

This would have normally triggered a trance in the subject. But it did not happen this time. Nambi therefore suspected that someone was interfering in his rite, and called out to ask whether there was any exorcist in the crowd. 'No,' Raother immediately answered. But his very voice betrayed him.

'In the end it might turn out that you are indeed an exorcist,' Nambi warned him.

Raother then left the place. In a while, as Nambi continued the rites, his abdomen began to bloat, and presently swelled up so much that he was hardly able to breathe. This was Raother's sorcery working on him. Nambi realised this, so he took a nail, muttered a mantra over it, and drove it into the trunk of a plantain tree in the compound. Immediately water began to gush out of the hole made by the nail, and Nambi's abdomen slowly regained its normal state, and he returned to the shed to resume the rites.

Presently Raother, confident of discomfiting his rival, returned to the place of exorcism. Aware of this, and wanting to teach Raother a lesson, Nambi took some holy ash in his palm and blew it into the crowd. Immediately all those on whom the ash fell, including Raother, began to hop about convulsively.

Unmindful of all this, Nambi continued his rites. In a while, the effect of the spell wore off on all except Raother—a giant of a man with an immense potbelly, he continued to bound about helplessly all by himself to the amusement of the crowd. Finally, near the point of physical collapse, he cried out to Nambi to release him from the spell and save his life.

'Who are you?' Nambi asked.

'I'm Usaka Raother,' Raother answered. 'Please forgive me. I did not know your power.'

'Raother? I've heard of you,' Nambi said. 'Please do come over here.'

These words of Nambi released Raother from the spell.

'You are a great exorcist,' Nambi told Raother as he shamefacedly stepped forward. 'Why don't you take over the rites now?'

'Please don't put me to further shame,' Raother pleaded. 'I won't be able to exorcize this woman, for I've cast a spell on her to prevent the Gandharvan from leaving her.'

'Of course you can exorcize her,' assured Nambi. 'There are counter-measures for all spells. All you've to do in this case is to put these flowers on her head.'

As soon as Raother did this, the woman went into a trance. He then, under Nambi's guidance, drove out the Gandharvan from her. And when her husband offered rewards to Nambi, he passed them on to Raother, saying that it was really he who drove out the spirit.

Reluctantly, Raother accepted the gifts. But he never forgave Nambi for the humiliation he had been made to suffer. And when he had an opportunity he took his revenge. This he did by sending Nambi an occult ring, which he said was in appreciation of Nambi's unique gifts. The moment he took the ring, Nambi knew he was trapped, and there was no escape. All he could do was trap Raother in turn, which he did by sending him a reply. 'This had to happen sometime or other,' he wrote. 'Now time and karma has converged. I have no regrets. But if it is forty for me, it is twelve for you.'

Raother died on the twelfth day, and Nambi on the fortieth.

The Grammar Lesson

Mahabhashyam, Patanjali's second century BC commentary on Panini's Sanskrit grammar, was once very nearly lost, according to a Kerala legend. The story is that one day, while Patanjali was teaching the text to his pupils, one of them got up and left the assembly without permission. This so enraged the violent-tempered sage that a great fireball shot out of his eyes and burned to ashes the entire group of students. But a moment later his anger turned into anguish, when he realized the enormity of what he had done—those students were the only ones who had learned his text, and he had destroyed them all!

Just then the truant student returned and, seeing what had happened, went up to the sage to console him, saying that he would preserve the sage's work as he had learned everything by heart. But once again the sage's eyes flashed in anger. 'You wretch! You're the cause of the death of all my dear disciples,' he yelled, and reduced him also to ashes.

So there was now no one at all to preserve his work. Fate had stolen his destiny, the great sage lamented, slumped in depression. Seeing this, a Gandharvan, who had been living on a banyan tree in the hermitage for some years, appeared before him, and said: 'I've been listening to all that you had taught, and have learned them all by heart. Please bless me and accept me as your disciple so that I may preserve your work.' Now once again Patanjali flared up, because the Gandharvan had learned his text secretly, without permission, and he cursed the handsome spirit to turn him into a hideous ogre. But later, on the Gandharvan's supplication, he relented and agreed to release him from the curse if he would find a deserving student and teach him *Mahabhashyam*.

The Gandharvan then resumed his perch on the banyan tree, and whenever a Brahmin youth passed by, he put a linguistic riddle to him, to test his suitability to learn *Mahabhashyam*. None passed the test for a long time. But finally a Brahmin youth from Kerala gave the correct answer, and was accepted by the Gandharvan as his disciple. For six uninterrupted months he then taught *Mahabhashyam* to the youth, during which he sat on the banyan tree and wrote the verses on its leaves and dropped them down, and the youth picked them up and memorized them. During this entire period, the youth did not sleep or rest or even eat, for the Gandharvan had given him a divine drug to prevent hunger and fatigue. When at last he had mastered the text perfectly, the Gandharvan blessed him and sent him on his way, but warned him that he should take care not to step into water, for that would reverse the effect of the drug given to him, and he would instantly fall asleep, from which he would not be able to wake up for six months. Then the Gandharvan departed, regaining his normal form, having been released from Patanjali's curse.

The youth too departed, carrying the bundle of manuscript leaves and minding the warning about not stepping into water. But after some months, when he came across a shallow rivulet, he momentarily forgot the warning, and, leaving the bundle of leaves on the river bank, stepped into the water to wash his face. The moment his feet touched water he collapsed. Fortunately, a young Sudra woman bathing nearby in the river, daughter of a local chieftain, saw this, and she got her servants to carry him to her home, thinking that he had fainted. She then summoned a physician, who, on examining the youth, said that he was only asleep, but added that if he did not wake up even after a day, she should rub his body with a paste of rice three times a day, so that he would not die for lack of nourishment.

For six months the youth slept, and during all this time the young woman lovingly nursed him. When he at last woke up, his first thought was about the safety of his manuscript bundle, and he rushed to the riverside to look for it. To his pleasant surprise he found the bundle still lying there, the leaves miraculously still green, and quite safe, except for a few leaves just then eaten by a cow. Even the leaves eaten by the cow he was able to recover undamaged the next morning from the dung of the cow.

Now he was ready to be on his way again. So he went to take leave of the woman who had saved his life, and offered to bless her with whatever she wished for as a reward. But she said that the only boon she desired was to be his wife. This put the youth in a quandary, for he had initially, before he met the Gandharvan, set out from his home to become an ascetic. He was reluctant to give up that goal. On the other hand, how could he possibly refuse the plea of the woman who had saved his life? A further complication was that by custom a Brahmin could take a Sudra wife only after first marrying a Brahmin, a Kshatriya and a Vaisya woman in succession. How could he, who had decided against any marriage at all, now marry four women?

These were the thoughts that passed through his mind. Finally he decided to fulfil his duties as a householder before taking sanyas. He then returned to his own home, married a woman from each of the three higher castes, and then married the Sudra woman. In time a son was born to each of his wives, and he taught them all *Mahabhashyam*. That, according to legend, was how the text came to be preserved.

POETIC JUSTICE

We are all creatures of chance. Frequently our lives take sudden and tortuous turns, often inexplicably, or because of some trivial incident. Life would be flowing tranquilly one moment, like a placid river on a gentle plain, only to cascade down a cliff the next moment, and turn viciously turbulent, its nature changed altogether.

Such was the transformation in the life of Vilyamangalathu Namboodiri. Born into an affluent and aristocratic family, he did not have a care in the world, and was ecstatically happy with the Sudra woman he had taken as his wife by sambandam marriage. But in just one night his life turned completely upside down, never to be the same again.

The Namboodiri's wife lived a couple of kilometres from his home, across a small river, but he was so enamoured of her that he never missed spending a night with her, whatever the difficulties of the day. The pivotal incident that turned his life in a new direction took place on a rainy winter night. The day had dawned clear and bright, but by noon it started to rain torrentially and incessantly. As the rain persisted even after nightfall, the Namboodiri began to fret, apprehensive that he might not be able to go to his wife that night. He waited for a while for the rain to subside, but as the night advanced, he decided to go to her anyhow, even though there was no let-up in the rain, and set out carrying an umbrella and a lighted torch of rolled coconut fronds.

It was pitch-dark outside, it being a new moon night. The umbrella was of little use because of the gusty wind, and soon his torch died out, drenched in the rain. Still he pressed on, feeling his way like a blind man. Somehow he got to the river bank. But the river, which normally had only knee-deep water, was now in flood, and there was no way he could wade across it. There was no ferryboat there, nor anyone around to help him to cross the river. Still the passion for his beautiful wife urged him on, and he scoured for some means to cross the river. Just then there was a flash of lightning, and he saw a tree-trunk lying on the river bank, and he blindly got on to it and somehow swam across the river. As he clambered ashore on the opposite bank, his feet got tangled in a rope, and, seeing that this was tied to the log, he fastened the free end of the rope to a tree, to prevent the log being swept away by the river, and proceeded to his wife's house.

It was past midnight by the time he got there. But his wife was still awake, reading a religious book and waiting for the Namboodiri, though she was doubtful whether he would come on such a night. When he called out to her, she immediately opened the door, and brought a towel for him to dry himself, and a change of clothes. After drying himself and changing his clothes, the Namboodiri went inside and sat on her bed, chewing the paan that she had prepared and regaling her with his adventures on the way.

She was pleased with his ardour, but was also upset by

what he told her, for she was a very pious woman, an ardent devotee of Krishna. 'How wonderful it would be if you were to show to the Lord the same devotion that you show towards me,' she said, pointing at the picture of Krishna hanging from the wall beside the bed. 'Isn't it a crime to waste your noble life in sensuality?'

As the Namboodiri turned his head and lifted his eyes to the picture, suddenly some light snapped on inside him, and the true purpose of his life was revealed to him in a flash. He sat absolutely still and silent for a while, his eyes riveted on the picture. 'You are right,' he said at last. 'I now know who I really am and what I should do.'

And while he sat there, his mind totally concentrated on Krishna, divine poetry began to well up within him, and this he went on reciting, as if in a trance. And as he recited the verses, the woman wrote them down. It seemed to her that Krishna in the picture on the wall nodded his head in approval of the poem, but not of all the verses, and she took down only those lines that Krishna approved. This, according to legend, was how the poetic masterpiece *Krishnamrtham* came to be composed. By daybreak the work was finished, and only then did the Namboodiri get up from his seat.

He rose without a word and left. On reaching the ford he looked for the tree-trunk he had secured there in the night, and to his horror found that what he had taken for a tree trunk in the night was in fact the corpse of a man. The rope was tied to its neck. Apparently, the man had committed suicide, and someone had flung the body into the river. The Namboodiri was dismayed at the thought that his passion had made him so blind as to mistake a corpse for a tree trunk. That strengthened his resolve to change his way of life.

On returning home, he performed an elaborate purification ceremony, and in a few days left home to become an ascetic. Later he became renowned as Vilyamangalathu Swamiyar.

There were no examinations to qualify doctors in ancient India—the guru's satisfaction was all that was required to mark the completion of medical studies. And each guru had his own method of judging the competence of his disciples. Some were hard to please, and this sometimes tried the patience of students. Thus Jivaka, the legendary physician of ancient India, when he was studying in Taxila, one day asked his guru, 'I learn much, and I learn easily; I understand well and do not forget what I have learned. I have now studied for seven years, but I do not see the end of this study. When will it end?'

And the guru said, 'Very well, Jivaka, take this spade and go around Taxila a *yojana* on every side, and whatever you see that is not of medicinal value, bring that to me.'

A couple of days later Jivaka returned and told the guru that he could not find anything that could not be used in medicine.

'Well then, you have mastered the medical science,' said the guru, acknowledging that Jivaka had learned that there is nothing on earth—plant, animal or material substance—

that is not of medicinal value, and that he had learned the properties of each item. With the blessing of his guru, Jivaka then returned to his home in Magadha, and went on to become the trusted physician of kings and sages, including Buddha.

Nineteenth century Kerala too had such a renowned physician, Vayaskara Narayanan Moossad. His remedies were often startlingly simple, requiring only the use of medicines prepared with the common plants found in any compound. Sometimes he prescribed no medicine at all, but cured patients with a simple regimen of diet or baths.

Typical of him was the way he cured the strange illness of a well-known lawyer, who suffered from incessant thirst, which could not be quenched however much water he drank, and had become utterly emaciated and weak. Various physicians had treated him, but with no effect, so he finally went to Vayaskara. On examining him, Moossad found that there was nothing seriously wrong with him, except that his body had become too dry. 'For twelve days every morning take an oil bath, and for your meals mix a good amount of ghee with rice,' advised Moossad. 'And at night drink a glass of milk. That is all the treatment you need.' And that cured the lawyer.

Kottarathil Sankunni, the compiler of the *Ithihyamala*, was himself once treated by Moossad. One day when Sankunni was bathing in a river, he had chest pain and constriction of breathing, and by the time he got back home he was in fever and had spasms of shivering. He then sent word to Moossad about his condition. Moossad thought about it for a moment, then said, 'If the problem arose while having a bath, then it must be cured by taking a bath,' and prescribed that Sankunni should take an oil bath every day

at noon for twelve days. The idea was turn to the potency of the illness against itself, like a jujitsu fighter using the strength of the opponent against him.

His treatment of yet another patient, who had been suffering from intermittent fever for six months, was also similar. 'Since you have been suffering from fever for six months, you must now take bath,' said Moossad, and told him to take an oil bath in hot water for fourteen days, and gave him a powder to rub on the scalp after drying his head thoroughly.

Narayanan Moossad was a grave and ascetic person, and his only weakness was a passion for Kathakali, which once made him work a trick cure on an artist. When the artist, who was to perform at Moossad's house one night, accidentally stepped on a fallen ear ornament and severely injured his foot, Moossad had an ointment applied to the wound so that it closed in a few hours, and he was able to perform as scheduled. But when the artist went to thank Moossad the next morning, Moossad told him that the cure he had effected was only temporary and that the wound would open again in a few days, and that it would take some three months for it to heal completely. And that was how it came to pass.

The Vayaskara Moossads never took fees for treating patients, however large the reward offered. Once a prominent British merchant in Kerala, whom Narayanan Moossad had cured of severe and persistent headache, sent him a thousand rupees—a princely sum those days—and an elephant as gifts, but Moossad politely refused to accept them, saying, 'Ours is a charitable service. We never accept any payment.'

Narayanan Moossad had the peculiar habit of never remaining in a house where the patient's death was imminent, or going to treat a patient whom he considered incurable, and once even refused to treat the raja of Travancore whose ailment he considered fatal. He had an almost supernatural ability to discern the signs of impending death, even in seemingly healthy persons. Once a Namboodiri arrived at Moossad's house bringing with him two of his grandchildren, a boy and a girl. Moossad examined the boy, who was suffering from chronic cough, and prescribed for him a simple medicine, powdered cumin and mustard seeds mixed with sugar. Then he turned to the girl and said, 'I don't know whether I can do anything for her.'

'She is not ill,' said the Namboodiri. 'She just came along for fun.'

Moossad looked sceptical but said nothing.

'Well, we should get going now,' said the Namboodiri, 'so we can reach home before nightfall.'

'Then start immediately,' said Moossad. 'There will be trouble at night.'

And the girl, who had seemed perfectly healthy in the day, died that very night.

Bhartrihari's Renunciation

Bhartrihari, the great seventh century Sanskrit poet, was, according to a legend popular in Kerala, prompted to take sanyas and write his celebrated renunciatory poems because of the faithlessness of his wife. The story is that a wizard once gave the poet a divine mango saying that it would bestow eternal youth on the person who ate it. The poet, thinking that it would be mean of him to remain youthful while his beautiful and beloved wife grew old and shrivelled, gave the mango to her, telling her about its unique potency.

Now it so happened that the woman, whom Bhartrihari believed to be chaste and entirely devoted to him, had a paramour, a servant of the poet, and she gave the mango to him, because she had no desire to live in eternal youth if her lover grew old and died. And he, with similar thoughts, gave it to his wife. This woman was a sweeper in the house, and Bhartrihari saw her leaving the house with the mango. So he called her to him and asked her where she got the mango, and she said that her husband gave it to her. He then grilled the man and got him to confess the truth.

The affair utterly disgusted Bhartrihari. But he decided

against making a fuss about it just then, so he let the man go and went into his room to lie down for a while and think about what he should do. 'What a shame it is that my wife, whom I loved dearly and trusted totally, should turn out to be just a common slut, keeping an ugly and low-caste servant as a lover,' he thought. He could not live with her any more, he decided.

Meanwhile the servant informed the poet's wife about what happened, and she, fearing that Bhartrihari would severely punish her lover and that she herself would be banished from the house, decided that the best solution to her predicament would be to kill her husband immediately. So she quickly prepared a plate of his favourite snacks, mixed some poison in it, and served it to him, saying that she had specially made it for him as there was a delay in getting the meal ready. Bhartrihari took the plate from her without expression, but suspecting what she was up to, put it aside. Then and there he decided not to stay in the house for another moment, and left immediately, to seek peace in sanyas.

For several months thereafter he wandered about the land, carrying an earthen begging bowl—his sole possession—and living on alms. Then he thought that it was not proper for him to go about begging, and resolved to live only on what people voluntarily offered him. Eventually he arrived at a famous temple (at Chidambaram, some say) and decided to remain there permanently. He took his seat at the western gate of the temple, as there was already a sanyasi seated at the eastern gate. He placed his begging bowl before him, and ate whatever food people dropped into it.

Some months later, a beggar one day approached the sanyasi at the eastern gate for alms. The sanyasi said that he had nothing to give, and suggested that he should seek alms from the rich sanyasi sitting at the western gate. When the beggar approached him, Bhartrihari told him that he too was a poor beggar and had nothing to give.

'But the sanyasi at the eastern gate told me that you are rich,' said the beggar.

Bhartrihari pondered over the significance of that charge, and realized that what the other sanyasi meant was that it was not proper for a true sanyasi to keep even a begging bowl, for the bowl implied that he was desirous of receiving alms. He therefore threw away the bowl, and thereafter received alms only in his palm.

It is said that Bhartrihari remained at the temple for the rest of his life and composed his poems of renunciation there, verses such as:

> *Blind in the inky night of passion*
> *I once had eyes only for women,*
> *But now with the dawn of wisdom,*
> *Brahman is all I see in all.*

Perumthachan, one of the twelve sons reputedly born of a low-caste woman to the sage Vararuchi and abandoned by him in various places in Kerala, was brought up by a carpenter. And he, like all his brothers who distinguished themselves in their particular professions, grew up to be a renowned architect and sculptor. And, again like most of his brothers, he was unconventional in his ways and something of a rebel.

The brothers, though they ignored class and caste distinctions when they met together once a year for the sradham rites of their father, observed caste taboos among themselves at other times, each being brought up in a different caste. So when Perumthachan one day went to visit Agnihotri, his Brahmin brother, he did not enter the compound, but stood waiting at the gate, as was expected of a man of his low caste. He had to wait for a long time, as Agnihotri was at his morning devotions.

'What rite is he performing?' Perumthachan asked Agnihotri's servant.

'Sahasravrthi,' said the servant.

Perumthachan then took out his chisel and dug a pit in the ground with it.

After a while he again asked the servant, 'What is he doing now?'

'He is worshipping Surya,' said the servant.

Again Perumthachan dug a pit.

Later, when he was told that Agnihotri was worshipping Ganesha, then too he dug a pit. And so it went on till noon, with Perumthachan digging a pit each time he was told that Agnihotri was performing a particular rite.

When at last Agnihotri came to the gate, Perumthachan asked, 'Are the rites all over?'

'Yes,' said Agnihotri. 'I'm sorry to have kept you waiting for so long. You would have got bored.'

'Not at all,' said Perumthachan. 'I kept myself busy digging these pits, one for each of the deities you worshipped. I am only disappointed that I could not reach water in any of them. Instead of digging so many pits, if I had spent the time digging just one pit I would have got water.'

Agnihotri realized that Perumthachan was ridiculing him for worshipping so many deities and implying that he should instead worship just one deity with total devotion. But Agnihotri had a ready response to that.

'Well,' he said, 'even if you dig many pits, if you dig them a little every day, in time you will find water in them all.'

'But the source of water in all the pits will be same,' returned Perumthachan.

'True,' conceded Agnihotri.

And Perumthachan said, 'As long as we don't forget that all divinity is one, we can worship any number of gods according to our fancy.'

There was a touch of playfulness in some of Perumthachan's

structures, as in the bridge he once built over a rivulet. He attached a wooden puppet to a mechanism at one end of the bridge, so that whenever a man climbed on to the bridge at the other end, the puppet would descend into the river, but would, by the time the man got to the opposite bank, rise to the top again with a mouthful of water which it would spray on the unwary man.

Seeing this trick, Perumthachan's son, who was even cleverer than his father, devised a counter-trick, and placed at the opposite end of the bridge a puppet of his own, which would advance in front of the man who walked on the bridge, and, drawing level to his father's puppet as it rose to the top, give it a slap on the face, so that the water it spewed would fall sideways, without soiling the man.

Perumthachan took this as a slap on his own face, and he watched his son's rapidly growing talent with desperate envy, fearing that his son's brilliance would put him in the shadow. Their rivalry ended in a terrible tragedy, in which Perumthachan, while he was working on a building, deliberately dropped a heavy chisel on his son working immediately below him, severing his head. And Perumthachan himself, chased by the local people, shut himself up in his house and set fire to it. He perished in the fire.

∾

Pride and Prejudice

It was a common practice among the kings and chieftains of ancient India to hold periodical conclaves of scholars and poets, to honour and reward those who distinguished themselves. This practice virtually died out in medieval times in most regions of India, but was continued in Kerala by some kings. Raja Manavikraman, a mid-fifteenth century Zamorin of Malabar, himself a distinguished scholar and author, was one such patron, who held a seven-day assembly of scholars once a year at the Tali temple in Kozhikode, his capital, at which participants were given 108 topics to debate, with a purse to be won in each topic.

The generosity of the raja attracted many scholars from all over Kerala, and even a few from the neighbouring regions, to participate in the conclave. The most distinguished of them was Uddanda Sastrikal, a headstrong savant from Tondaimandalam in the Tamil country, who arrived trumpeting:

Flee, O flee, you wretched, elephantine poets,
Here comes Uddanda, the lion of Vedanta!

Uddanda indeed proved invincible, and year after year for many years he won all the purses. He thus became a favourite of the king, and took up his residence in the palace. This was a matter of shame to local scholars, not to speak of substantial pecuniary loss to them. But there was nothing that they could do about it, for none of them had the scholarship or the debating skill to get the better of Uddanda. To defeat Uddanda they needed a new scholar to rise among them. So when they heard that the wife of one of them had conceived, they performed various rites and fed the woman with specially sanctified butter daily throughout her pregnancy, praying for a talented child to be born to her, capable of ousting Uddanda for his seat of eminence.

The child that was born in answer to their prayers and rites was Kakkasseri Bhattathiri. A boy of extraordinary intelligence and keenness of observation, he learned to read and write when he was just three years old, and was initiated into the study of the Vedas at the age of five, instead of at the usual age of seven or eight. In a short time Kakkasseri mastered all the traditional knowledge and became a forceful debater. He was then taken to Kozhikode to participate in the annual assembly of scholars.

Uddanda was amused that a mere boy should presume to challenge him, but soon his amusement turned into consternation, when every proposition that he formulated was systematically demolished by Kakkasseri, arguing his case with authority and unerring logic.

The discomfiture of his favourite courtier upset the raja, and he sought to save Uddanda's face by ruling that the debate was a tie, and that whoever gave the greatest number of explanations for the first stanza of *Raghuvamsa*, the epic poem of Kalidasa, would be declared the winner. Uddanda was an unrivalled authority on the epic, and the raja was confident that no one would be able to best him in that subject. Relieved, Uddanda proceeded to give an elaborate exposition of the meaning of the stanza, interpreting it in four different ways. But to his dismay Kakkasseri gave eight different equally convincing interpretations. Uddanda then gracefully admitted defeat.

The two scholars met again several times in different places, and on all those occasions it was Kakkasseri who won the debates. Meanwhile, Kakkasseri also wrote an acclaimed Sanskrit play titled *Vasumati-Manavikrama*, about the Zamorin and his queen. All this made him famous and a hero among Kerala Brahmins.

But they also had reason to be apprehensive about Kakkasseri, because of his lack of respect for Brahminical conventions, and his growing tendency to be salacious and irreverent in his comments. Kakkasseri contemptuously disregarded caste taboos and mixed freely with people of all castes, even ate food in the company of low-caste men. Brahmins therefore considered him a threat to their way of life, and wanted to ostracize him as an outcaste. But none dared to confront him, for fear that he would argue his way out of the charges levelled against him. It was clear that they could not do anything against Kakkasseri without his acquiescence.

In this quandary, a few orthodox Brahmins one day accosted Kakkasseri and asked him: 'What should we do in our predicament?'

And Kakkasseri, knowing what they meant, answered: 'Fall at the feet of Devi.'

'What would be the result?' they asked.

'That'll humble even Brahma,' Kakkasseri replied.

The Brahmins then gathered together in a building and decided to follow Kakkasseri's advice, and for forty-one days they worshipped Devi uninterruptedly. On the last day of the rites Kakkasseri arrived there, and asked for a drink of water without entering the building. One of the Brahmins brought him a tumbler of water. Kakkasseri took it and drank some water from it, then placed it upside down on the floor, and said, 'I've become an outcaste. I'll not hereafter enter your homes or temples, or touch any of you.'

Saying this, he abruptly turned and left. It is not known where he went or what happened to him, or how his life ended.

A Bridal Mismatch

Oracles were at one time as common in Kerala as astrologers would be in later times. But they, unlike conventional astrologers, did not depend on horoscopic calculations, but made their predictions intuitively, according to the potency of the time of consultation, and the appearance, words and gestures of the subject. Often their divinations were uncannily accurate.

Mangalapilly Moothath of Thiruvalla in southern Kerala was one such blessed oracle. A Potti once approached him with the horoscopes of a number of girls for choosing a bride. Moothath rapidly scanned the horoscopes, dropping them one after the other on the floor with barely a glance at them, saying that they were not suitable. Finally he held out one horoscope and told Potti, 'This girl is ideal for you. But you'll not be able to marry her.'

Potti took the horoscope from Moothath and, noting the identity of the girl, said: 'I don't think there'll be any difficulty in marrying her. Our families are related. Besides we are on very friendly terms with the girl's parents.'

'We'll see,' said Moothath.

'I'm confident,' said Potti.

'Then go ahead and arrange it,' said Moothath. 'But I don't think you'll be able to marry her. And the girl you marry will die within six months of the wedding. You'll have to marry again to beget children.'

Potti was not convinced. And, as he expected, when he approached the girl's father for her hand, he readily agreed to it. All matters concerning the wedding were quickly and amicably settled, and the date and muhoortham (auspicious time) for the ceremony fixed. There was not even the faintest hint of anything amiss as the preparations for the wedding got under way. Moothath evidently had been proved wrong.

But on the wedding day, when the rites were about to begin, a minor altercation between two guests suddenly and unexpectedly flared into a raging row, with guests and relatives splitting into two groups, one group insisting on performing the marriage, and the other vehemently opposing it. In this predicament, the girl's father said to the group opposed to the marriage, 'What am I to do if you fight like this? I've to give my daughter in marriage. If you say that I should not give her to Potti, then tell me what I should do?'

Hearing this, a young man of the group stepped forward. 'I'll marry her,' he said. 'And I'll marry her without any dowry. If you agree, I'll right away go and take a ritual bath and return, so the ceremony can be performed at the fixed muhoortham.' The girl's father had no alternative but to agree.

As Potti stood bewildered and mortified by this development, the leader of his group went up to him and said, 'Don't you worry. I'll give you my daughter in marriage, and will give you double the dowry these people have offered. Are you ready?'

In the confusion of the moment, Potti agreed to this, forgetting the oracle's warning, and the wedding was performed the same day, at the very same muhoortham fixed for his wedding with the other girl.

But true to Moothath's prediction, the bride died soon after the marriage. So once again Potti approached Moothath with a bundle of horoscopes to select a bride.

'Everything happened as I predicted, no?' Moothath asked. 'And now you want to marry again?'

'Yes,' said Potti apologetically. 'I have a few horoscopes here. Please examine them carefully at your convenience and advise me whom I should marry.'

'I'll tell you right away,' said Moothath. 'There's no need for me to examine the horoscopes. My practice is to say whatever comes to my mind. By divine grace most of my predictions come true.'

'I've full faith in you,' said Potti.

'From the bundle, remove the first two horoscopes and take the third. It'll be of a girl born under the star Karthika. She's a good match for you. Out of this marriage two boys and a girl will be born to you. Her fourth pregnancy will end in miscarriage, and she will not conceive again. That's all you need to know now.'

And all that came true.

❧

A Yakshi and Her Lover

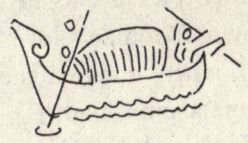

In classical Sanskrit the term *devanam-priya*, meaning 'beloved of the gods', also meant 'simpleton', for these innocents were forever blessedly happy, untouched by the travails of life. This was how it was with Venmani Namboodiri, a boarder in a Vedic school in Thrissur. He was the butt of all sorts of pranks of his schoolmates, but bore them all with gawky cheerfulness.

But one day they went a little too far. That day, when they were at the main temple of the town for their morning devotions, they made Venmani stand before the painting of a yakshi (a demi-goddess) on the wall of the sanctum and pray that she should visit him that night. That was a dangerous prank, for a real yakshi, enchanted by the beauty of the portrait, had merged into the painting. And she, seeing the young men visiting the temple daily, had developed a craving to cohabit with them, and had taken to spending the night with the men she fancied, assuming the form of an ethereally beautiful woman. Also, she never refused anyone's request to sleep with him.

The coitus with the yakshi was indeed divine, but few

had the strength to survive it. Often the men she slept with were found dead in the morning. So the boys were really playing with Venmani's life by inducing him to make the wish before the yakshi painting. But Venmani, though weak in the head, was otherwise well-endowed and potent, and the yakshi found him irresistible in bed. No man, it seemed, had given her as much pleasure as he did. And Venmani, who had never known a woman's love before, was ecstatic with the yakshi. So, when at dawn she rose to depart, he asked, 'Will you come again tonight?'

'If you wish,' said the yakshi. 'Not only tonight but every night. But on one condition . . .'

'Tell me.'

'You shouldn't touch any other woman without my permission,' she said. 'If you do, I'll never again come to you.'

Venmani readily agreed to that condition; he had no desire for any other woman, anyway. Their happy liaison thus went on smoothly for several months. Then one day Venmani's father arrived at the school to inquire about him, and finding that he had made no progress in studies, decided to take him back home the next morning. This threw Venmani into confusion, for fear that he would now lose the yakshi.

'What shall I do?' he asked her when she visited him that night.

'Don't worry,' the yakshi said. 'I'll visit you at home.'

So their intimacy continued. But after a while there was yet another problem—the youth's father wanted him to get married. Venmani, remembering the yakshi's warning that she would stop visiting him if he slept with another woman, tried to wriggle out of the situation by informing his father through a relative that he did not wish to get married. His father would not agree to that.

'I wish to see a grandson born, so this family will not die out,' he told the youth. 'That's why you should marry.'

'Whatever you say, I won't marry,' the youth swore. 'Please don't compel me.'

'That's thoughtless and irresponsible,' said his father. 'Tell me why you don't want to marry.'

'No particular reason,' said Venmani. 'I just don't want to marry.'

'How dare you say this to me!' his father flared up. 'Get out of my sight right now, and stay out of my sight. I don't want to see you ever again.'

When Venmani told the yakshi of his predicament that night, she said: 'We will make a compromise. You go ahead and marry, but you should sleep with your wife only on alternate nights. On the other nights you should sleep with me.'

Venmani was delighted with the arrangement, and first thing in the morning he went and apologized to his father for his obstinacy and told him that he had changed his mind. In a short while he married a girl his father chose for him, and by and by she gave birth to a son. Everything thus worked out to everybody's satisfaction. But when the child grew up and the time for his upanayanam arrived, there was yet another crisis. When Venmani told the yakshi of the ceremony, she said, 'I've a wish—when the boy seeks alms as part of the ritual, I should be the first one to give him alms.'

'That'll be no problem,' he said confidently. As his parents had passed away a few years earlier, he could, as the head of the family, now decide what should be done.

On the day of the ceremony the yakshi took the form of a Brahmin housewife and arrived at the house with some rice in a bowl. This caused considerable confusion among the assembled relatives, for no one knew who she was or why she had come.

'The boy should first seek alms from this woman who has just arrived,' Venmani told the boy's designated guru, who was also the priest at the rite. 'After that his mother can give him alms.'

'That's not proper,' objected the priest. 'The boy should first seek alms from his mother, only then from others.'

'This woman is the boy's elder mother,' responded Venmani. 'She's my first wife.'

Everyone was aghast at the confession, and it led to an altercation among the guests, with many questioning the truthfulness of Venmani's claim. And his wife, frenzied with anger, declared: 'From where has this she-devil come all dressed up? I'll drive her out of the house with a broom.'

'Please don't do anything rash,' Venmani pleaded helplessly. 'You don't know who you're dealing with.'

No one heeded him. In the ensuing fracas, his wife caught hold of the yakshi and, with the help of a few other women, dragged her out of the house. The yakshi then assumed her true form and said to Venmani: 'I don't blame you for any of this. But after this humiliation I can't come here any more.' Saying this, she disappeared heavenward in a streak of light.

∾

The Hakim and the Vaidya

Physicians in India enjoyed a high social status in early Vedic times, when priests doubled as healers. But later, when caste taboos hardened, the physician's profession came to be considered defiling, since he came into contact with people of all castes. 'A Brahmin must not practise medicine, for the physician is impure, unfit for sacrifice,' warned the *Taittiriya-samhita*, a late Vedic text.

This proscription was, however, ignored by Namboodiris, the highest class of Kerala Brahmins, who dominated the medical profession in Kerala well into modern times. But in some parts of Kerala, especially in north Malabar, hakims (Muslim physicians practising the Unani system of medicine, an amalgam of Greek and Arabian traditions) gained prominence in the late medieval period. As a result, medical knowledge among Hindus in Malabar declined.

In this quandary, a few Brahmin leaders held consultations among themselves and decided that somehow they should acquire medical knowledge from hakims. For this they devised a plan, to depute one among them to study medicine under a hakim by assuming the guise of a Muslim youth.

The man chosen for this task was Vakbhattan, a bright and personable youth in his twenties. With the blessings of his elders, he then put on the Muslim dress, wore a cap and approached an eminent hakim of the region for instruction.

Now it so happened that this physician was a rich and generous patron of medical studies, who had under him a number of disciples, to whom he provided free board and lodge and even gave stipends for their daily expenses. He took no fees from anyone. When Vakbhattan approached him, he agreed to take him as a disciple, deeming him to be a Muslim youth. 'If you're diligent and clever, I'll teach you,' said the hakim. 'I've no time for dull or lazy people.'

Vakbhattan easily passed the eligibility test, but he politely declined the offer of board and lodge and stipend. 'I've a relative across the river,' he said. 'I'll stay there. You don't have to give me any stipend either. All I seek is knowledge.'

The answer pleased the physician. 'As you wish,' he said.

Vakbhattan turned out to be a star pupil, and the hakim grew so fond of him that one day he made an unusual offer to him. 'If you desire, I'm willing to teach you even at night,' he said. 'You can come back here after your evening meal.' The youth was happy with the offer, as he was keen to complete his studies as quickly as possible and return to his fold.

The nightly lessons were given in the hakim's bedroom, and exclusively to Vakbhattan, with the physician lying in bed and giving instruction, and the disciple sitting on the floor and learning. Often the lessons went on until daybreak, as the teacher thought that he should stop only when the student said that he was weary, and the student thought that he could not stop until the teacher said that it was enough for the day.

Soon Vakbhattan mastered all the texts that the hakim

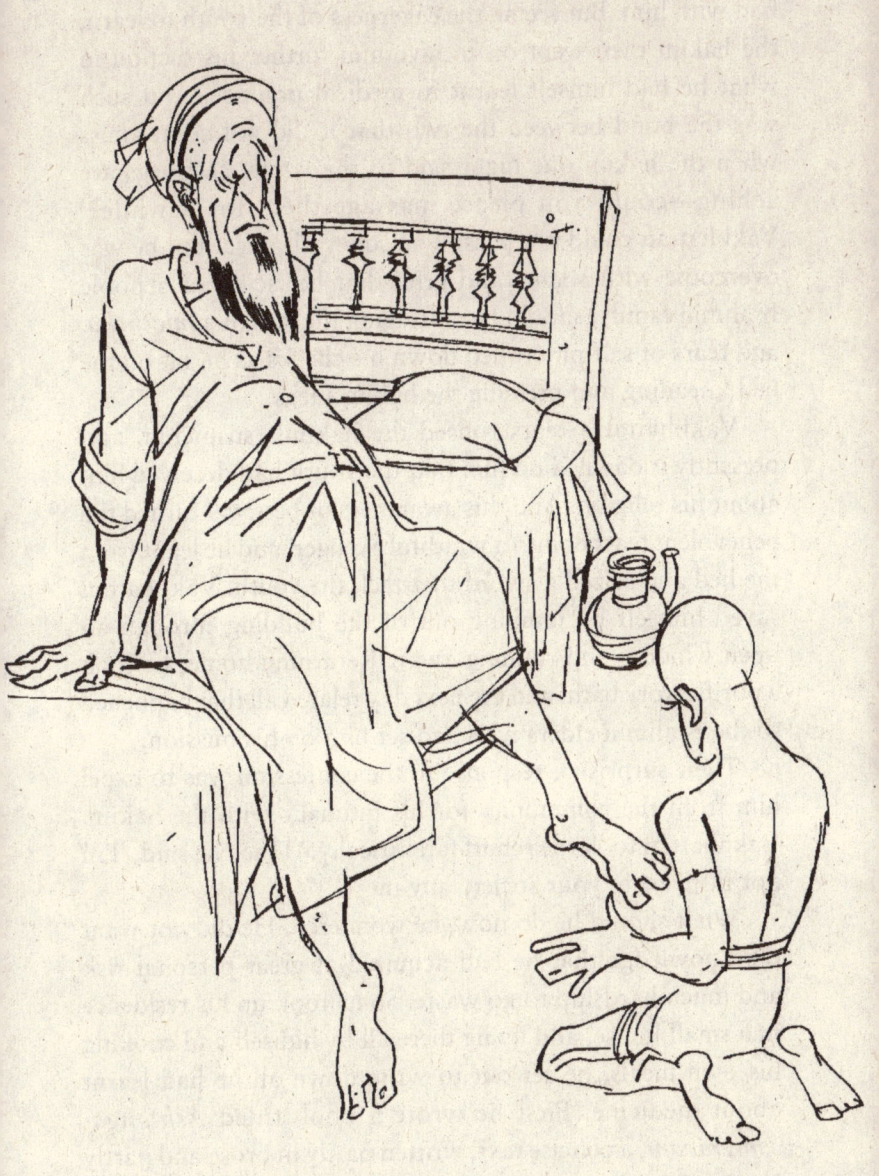

had with him. But seeing the eagerness of the youth to learn, the hakim then went on to give him further instruction in what he had himself learnt in medical practice. And such was the bond between the two that it did not seem amiss when the hakim one night said to the youth, 'My legs are aching—could you please massage them for a while?' Vakbhattan could not possibly disobey his guru. But he was overcome with shame and grief that he, scion of a noble Brahmin family, should be massaging the legs of a *mlechcha*, and tears of self-pity rolled down his cheeks as he sat on the bed kneading and pressing the hakim's legs.

Vakbhattan's tears roused the hakim's suspicion, and presently it dawned on him that the youth had deceived him about his religion. And this awareness of betrayal turned the benevolent teacher into a wrathful avenger, and he leapt from the bed and seized a sword to attack the youth. Vakbhattan saved himself by jumping out of the building through an open window and running away. Returning home, he took a purificatory bath, and the next day related all that happened to the Brahmin elders who had set him on his mission.

Their surprising response to the confession was to expel him from the community for his intimacy with the hakim. Vakbhattan took the rebuff fatalistically. 'True,' he said, 'I'm not fit to be in your society any more.'

What should he do now, he wondered. He did not want the knowledge that he had acquired at great personal risk and much hardship to go waste. So he took up his residence in a small house, and living there all by himself and cooking his own meals, he set out to write down all he had learnt about medicine. First he wrote a book titled *Ashtanga-samgraham*, a concise text, written partly in prose and partly in verse. But he was not happy with it, so he wrote a more condensed version of the text all in verse that could be easily learnt by heart, and yet again a third book summarizing the essence of other well-known medical texts. He presented the three books to the Brahmin elders, and left the place, and was never again seen.

The conclave of Brahmins discussed at length whether they could accept the texts written by an ostracized person. They finally decided to accept them, but with the stipulation that these texts should not be studied on the ekadasi day, the day of austerities marking the eleventh day of the lunar month.

Tantric Miracles

In early medieval times, when Hinduism froze into its orthodox mould, unorthodox sectaries like Tantrics had to retreat to the outlying regions of India, like Kerala, Bengal and Kashmir. Kerala had a good number of Tantrics at this time, and one of the most renowned of them was Puliambilly Namboodiri of north Malabar, whose reputation for miraculous powers was such that many families took to venerating him as a household deity after his death, and this practice continued even into the twentieth century.

Puliambilly was an ardent devotee of Kali. And, though born into an orthodox Brahmin family, he was a practitioner of Tantric rites, which involved drinking alcohol, eating meat and fish, and ritual sexual intercourse.

These practices of Puliambilly were abhorrent to conservative Namboodiris, and they sought to condemn him as an outcaste. But to do that they needed direct evidence of his practices, and that was difficult to obtain, for Puliambilly performed the Tantric rites only at home and at night, behind closed doors. But one day, on reliably learning that he had gone to buy toddy for his rites, they intercepted him on his way home with a pot of toddy on his head.

'What's in the pot?' they asked with seeming innocent curiosity.

Puliambilly immediately knew what they were up to, but decided to play along for a while. He demurred to answer, pretending to be uneasy. That convinced the Namboodiris that it was indeed toddy in the pot. Besides, the rank smell of toddy pervaded the air.

'Come on, tell us,' they insisted.

'It's nothing special,' said Puliambilly, assuming a downcast, guilty look.

'We want to see,' they said, and by force took down the pot and placed it on the ground.

'What's this foul smell from the pot?' they asked. 'Untie the cover—we want to see what's in the pot.'

'It's just boiled areca,' Puliambilly said evasively.

'Really?' said the Namboodiris. 'Let's see.'

'If you insist,' said Puliambilly, untying its cover.

And indeed it turned out that the pot was really full of areca. As the bewildered Namboodiris looked on, Puliambilly carefully retied the cover of the pot, placed it on his head, and went on home. When the time for his puja arrived, areca became toddy again.

The Namboodiris were now at a loss about how to deal with Puliambilly. Eventually they decided to seek the help of the local raja to punish the Tantric for violating caste rules. The raja told them that if they could tell him for certain when Puliambilly would be performing Tantric rites, he would arrange to catch him at it. They informed him that Puliambilly would be certainly performing the rites on the new-moon night of Karkadakam (July–August), and so it was decided to trap him that night.

On the designated night the Namboodiris assembled at the palace, and the raja sent a messenger to summon Puliambilly to the court. On arriving at the Tantric's house, the messenger informed Puliambilly's wife, through a servant woman of the house, about the raja's order. Puliambilly was at this time lying in a drunken stupor after puja, and when he was told of the royal summons by his wife, he dismissively said, 'It's too dark now. I'll go when the moon rises.'

The messenger carried the reply to the palace, and everybody had a good laugh over it, knowing that the moon would not be seen on the new-moon night. But as it was too late in the night to do anything about Puliambilly that day, the raja retired to his bedchamber, and the Namboodiris went to sleep in the gatehouse of the palace.

Meanwhile Puliambilly woke up with a vague recollection of the royal summons, and asked his wife about it. When she told him about his impudent reply, he felt uneasy about its possible consequences, and decided to go to the palace immediately, trusting that Kali would save him from the raja's wrath.

And indeed, she did, for as he stepped out of the house, a full moon miraculously rose over the horizon. So on reaching the palace, he confidently went up to the raja's bedchamber and knocked on the door.

'Who's it?' the raja demanded.

'It's I, Puliambilly.'

'What? Has the moon risen?' the raja asked.

'Yes, indeed,' said Puliambilly. 'Come out and look.'

Seeing the miracle, the raja, instead of condemning Puliambilly, summoned the Namboodiris, and in their abashed presence conferred many honours on him. The Tantric then returned home. And the moment he entered the house, the full moon also disappeared, for it was an illusion created by Kali to save her devotee.

Because of his intense devotions, Kali used to appear in person before Puliambilly, though she remained invisible to others. But he later lost that favour. This happened one night when he, accompanied by Kali, was returning home after an exorcism rite. Along the way she suddenly disappeared, but on searching, he found her in an outcaste Paryan's hut, receiving his oblations, though remaining invisible to him. This upset Puliambilly, and when Kali returned to him after the puja, he protested about it, saying that it was improper for her to favour the devotions of an untouchable who had no knowledge of tantram and mantram.

And Kali said, 'You still don't know my true nature, do you? I make no distinction between Chandalas and Brahmins. Wherever devotees call me, I go there, whoever they are. I value devotion far more than tantram and mantram. Since you have not yet understood this, you will never again be able to see me in person. But if you keep on worshipping me with devotion, I will continue to show favours to you.' Saying this, she instantly disappeared.

The Lost Purse

It was common and entirely respectable for poor Brahmins in Kerala to seek, in times of dire need, charitable gifts from rajas, chieftains and other rich people. And people were generally glad to help them, considering it to be a pious deed. So when a poor Namboodiri of Vanneri in north Malabar was at a loss to find money to marry off his daughters, he naturally decided to go on a tour to seek gifts.

The mission took him to every corner of Kerala, and he was able to collect, over a couple of months, a good amount of money, enough to marry off his daughters. Then he set out for home. On the way, weary and hungry, he stopped one day at the Killikurissimangalam temple near Kozhikode, to have a meal and rest for a while.

'Are the noon rituals over?' he asked the temple priest.

'Yes,' said the priest. 'But if you go and have a bath quickly, you can eat with us.'

At the temple tank the Namboodiri removed the cloth purse he had tied around his waist and placed it on the ground, and then stepped into the pool to say the customary prayers and to take a quick dip. But when he emerged from the tank, he found to his dismay that the purse was gone, even though he had been in the tank only for a very short time. He then ran to the temple and raised an alarm, but no one there had seen anyone approach the tank. A further search around the tank also proved futile. The loss of the purse so grieved the Namboodiri that, though famished, he could barely eat the meal his solicitous hosts served him. He then lay down in the temple and slept for a while, having no strength to go on. Waking up later, he resigned himself to his fate, and left for his home village.

But there was still the unresolved problem of having to find money to marry off his daughters. So a few months later he again set out from home to seek charity. On the way, he once again stopped at the Killikurissimangalam temple, to spend the night there. The priest recognized him immediately and gently ribbed him, asking, 'You aren't going to lose your purse this time, are you?'

'Not this time,' the Namboodiri laughed. 'For that I'll come again after I've collected money. I'm only just now setting out on my journey.'

He had his meal at temple, and asked the priest where he could find a place to sleep.

'You can come with me,' said the priest. 'There's plenty of room in the house where I sleep.'

The priest then took the Namboodiri to the nearby house of Kalakkath Nambiar, where he had a sambandam liaison with a woman of the house. The woman greeted them with water to wash their feet and spread a grass mat in the veranda of the inner courtyard of the house for them to sit. She then placed an oil lamp before them and served them a tray of paan.

The two Brahmins sat there in the flickering light of the

oil lamp, chewing paan and exchanging banter. And the woman stood near them, listening. In the course of their conversation, the priest remarked about the sad plight of the Nambiar family, as only girls had been born there for a long time. The Namboodiri then regaled them with stories about his efforts to marry off his daughters, and mentioned the incident of losing his purse at the temple tank. Hearing this, the woman asked a few questions about the incident, then went into the strong-room of the house and brought out a cloth purse and placed it before the Namboodiri.

'Is this the purse you lost?' she asked.

'Yes, indeed,' said the astounded Namboodiri. 'Even my knot has not been untied.'

He then opened the purse and counted the money. Nothing was missing. 'How did you get this?' he asked the woman.

'I had gone to the temple tank that afternoon for a bath, and saw there a pile of cow dung on the ground. As I scooped it up, I found this purse underneath it,' said the woman. 'I brought it home, cleaned it and kept it in a chest, thinking that I would return it if anyone came to claim it. I was uneasy about keeping it. But now I'm relieved.'

The Namboodiri now remembered that he had seen a cow grazing nearby when he was in the tank, and had indeed seen the cow dung pile itself, but it did not occur to him to look under it for his purse. He now divided the money in the purse into two equal parts, and offered one part to the woman, saying, 'This is like a free gift to me now, so I would like you to have half of it.'

'No,' said the woman. 'I don't want even a paisa. It is virtuous to return a lost property to its owner, but to seek to gain from it is sinful. Had I wanted, I could've kept all the money for myself. All I seek is your blessing.'

Touched by the integrity of the woman, the Namboodiri rose from his seat, placed both his hands on the woman's head and blessed: 'A son will be born to you within a year from now, a most brilliant child.'

And that was how it came to be. The boy that was born to the woman was Kunjan Nambiar, the renowned eighteenth century Malayalam poet.

Kochunni: Outlaw

Kayamkulam, on the eastern bank of a broad lagoon in southern Kerala, is today a sleepy, nondescript little town, but in the mid-nineteenth century the region around it was a dreaded outlaw country, for it was the playground of Kayamkulam Kochunni, the legendary Robin Hood-like bandit of Kerala.

Kochunni was born at midnight on the new-moon day of Karkadakam (July–August) in 1818. His father too was a thief, but not a particularly successful one, so the family was in desperate straits most of the time. Unable to bear the privation, Kochunni fled from home to a nearby town when he was about ten years old. There he came under the care of a kindly Brahmin. When Kochunni told the Brahmin that he was a poor Muslim boy who had left home because of starvation, the man gave him a bowl of rice-gruel to eat, and later arranged for him to be employed in a large general store in the town. Kochunni would never forget that act of kindness, and would always remain protective towards that Brahmin family, even in the midst of his most virulent depredations.

Kochunni was initially employed in the store as a menial, and was given only food and shelter, but no wages. However, seeing the boy's diligence and alertness at work, the shopkeeper gradually, over a period of two or three years, increased his responsibilities, and granted him a modest monthly salary, in addition to providing him food and shelter. Kochunni faithfully handed over his salary to his parents every month, without spending any money on himself.

Around this time a Thangal (Muslim headman) set up a kalari in Kayamkulam. Hearing about it, Kochunni one day went to him and requested him to take him also as a student. The Thangal bristled at the suggestion. 'Your father became a robber even without any martial training,' said the Thangal. 'Now, if I teach you, you'll become an even more dangerous criminal. The art I teach is only for self-defence, not for harming anyone. I won't teach you.'

Kochunni was not disheartened by the rebuff. And he found a way around it. The Thangal held his classes late in the evening, so every day, after his shop closed, Kochunni would sneak to Kayamkulam and hide near the kalari, to watch and learn the exercises that the Thangal taught to his students. When the Thangal came to hear of this, he called Kochunni to him and asked, 'I hear that you've been secretly watching and learning the exercises—what have you learned?'

'Everything,' said Kochunni boldly.

'Show me,' said the Thangal

To the amazement of Thangal, the boy turned out to be far more proficient than all his disciples. So he took him in as a regular student. And, recognizing Kochunni's keenness and talent, the Thangal privately taught him many secret skills—such as assuming disguises and remaining invisible to others—which he did not deem fit to teach his other students.

Meanwhile Kochunni also learned to read and write with help of the clerks in the shop.

This phase of Kochunni's life ended when the shopkeeper came to hear about his martial arts exploits, and perhaps also about his family background. He therefore decided that it would not be proper for him to employ Kochunni any more. 'You're now about twenty years old, and you've acquired many skills,' he said to Kochunni. 'It's now time for you to look for other means of livelihood. You've been a great help to me all these years, and I'll never forget it. Hereafter too, I'll help you in whatever manner I can, and you should also help me when I'm in need.' He then settled Kochunni's account, paid him all his dues, and sent him off with his blessings.

Kochunni returned home to his parents. Soon, he married, and later, when his parents passed away, brought his mother-in-law to live with him. And gradually, as he had no other means of livelihood, Kochunni organized a gang of his own and took to robbery, looting houses and waylaying travellers. But he never robbed the poor, or anyone who had ever helped him in any way. He had a unique and courteous way of extorting money—on identifying the victim, usually an exploitative rich man, he would go to the man's house and ask for a certain amount of money as a loan. If the man obliged, Kochunni would not trouble him thereafter, and sometimes would even repay with interest the amount given. Most people gave him what he asked, as protection money. Refusal to pay him was a virtual invitation to Kochunni to plunder the house, which he invariably did within a week.

Kochunni was a handsome and strapping young man, broad-shouldered and deep-chested, with a clear, golden complexion and long bright eyes under beautifully arched eyebrows. His voice was soft and his speech gentle. He never used violence if he could possibly avoid it. And he was ever ready to help the poor and the needy, without any regard to caste or religion. He was careless with money, and lived with no thought of the future. Whatever money he got, he spent it promptly, or gave it away to the needy. Consequently he never accumulated wealth, though most of his more prudent associates eventually became men of substance.

Although a thief, Kochunni was in every other way a very decent, honourable, even compassionate, man. He had, in his long career of crime, killed only three persons, and these crimes were not related to his profession as a bandit. They were crimes of passion, committed in the heat of the moment, without deliberation.

Kochunni's only weakness was an inordinate fondness for sex, and there were many women in his life. He was especially fond of a Sudra woman, on whom he showered opulent gifts, neglecting his own family. This was strongly resented by his wife and mother-in-law, particularly by his mother-in-law, and it often led to bitter quarrels at home. One day Kochunni got so furious at the incessant nagging of his mother-in-law that he hit her hard on the head with a truncheon. That silenced her. Forever.

Kochunni rolled the corpse in a mat, tied a heavy stone to it and sank it secretly in the lagoon. But the secret was soon out and became a subject of common talk in Kayamkulam, and this for the first time brought Kochunni to the attention of police officials. They had till then generally ignored Kochunni's crimes, for banditry was an everyday occurrence in that age of lawlessness in Kerala. Murder was a different matter.

The authorities now ordered Kochunni's arrest, and he

went into hiding. But he did not give up his depredations—indeed, he now widened his field of operations into the neighbouring districts, so it became impossible for the small police force in the region to keep track of him or seize him, especially as Kochunni now moved about with great caution. The police moreover were afraid to confront him directly, as he was a fierce fighter and was always armed with a long dagger.

Kochunni remained free for some ten years after he was declared an outlaw. This was a matter of acute embarrassment to the government, so the diwan of Travancore issued a peremptory order to the tashildar (local administrator) of Kayamkulam to arrest Kochunni within a week or face dismissal from service. The tashildar then decided to use a stratagem to capture Kochunni. Learning that Kochunni's Sudra mistress had another lover of her own caste, the tashildar secretly contacted him, and with his help enticed the woman, with a promise of rich reward, to drug Kochunni when he visited her.

Her opportunity came the very next day, for around midnight that day Kochunni arrived at her cottage. As he washed his hands and feet and went into the bedroom, she gave him a glass of hot milk mixed with the drug given by the tashildar. He took it without hesitation, for it was her practice to give him a glass of milk before getting into bed with him. The moment he drank the milk, he fell unconscious. Then, on a signal from the woman, the policemen hiding nearby came and bound him tightly and carried him to the lock-up. There they chained his arms and legs, and sent word to the tashildar about the arrest, and he in turn sent a message about it to the diwan.

The tashildar rejoiced too soon. The following morning

Kochunni regained consciousness, and found himself in the lock-up. He remained quiet all through the day, seemingly resigned to his fate. But that night he smashed the chains binding him—with the connivance of policemen, it was rumoured—and escaped. He went straight to the cottage of his Sudra mistress, and there he found the woman happily dallying with her other lover, certain that Kochunni would be either executed or exiled by the government. His sudden appearance threw them into numb dread, and they cowered in a corner of the room. Kochunni's immediate concern was to retrieve the dagger that he had placed under the woman's bed the previous night. He now took it and turned on the faithless woman and her lover, and with a fiendish blow severed both their heads.

Then he went to his own house. In contrast to the celebratory scene he saw in his mistress's house, here he found his faithful wife sitting up awake without food or water and mourning for him. Kochunni consoled her, and resolved never again to be unfaithful to her. But he could not stay there, for the police had by then mounted a massive manhunt for him.

News of Kochunni's escape from the police lock-up and his murder of the Sudra woman and her lover spread like wildfire through the countryside, and in popular imagination he became something of a superman, capable of the most impossible feats. The police, despite all their efforts, could find no trace of him. It was thought that he had fled the land, for Kochunni remained in hiding and was inactive for a while. But soon he and his gang resumed their banditry, and with such brazen daredevilry that it became dangerous for people to travel through the Kayamkulam region, by land or by water. Kochunni was even bold enough to keep visiting his wife regularly, and three sons and a daughter were born to him during this period.

He lived as an outlaw for some eighteen years, eluding all efforts of the police to capture him. But when Sir Madhavarayar took over as the diwan of Travancore, he set the restoration of law and order in the kingdom as his primary objective, and appointed a new tashildar in Kayamkulam with the specific order to somehow arrest Kochunni. The local police then launched yet another vigorous effort to capture him, but again they failed. Finally the tashildar managed to bribe one of Kochunni's close associates, and induced him to betray Kochunni by plying him with drugged savouries.

So once again Kochunni found himself in the police lock-up. This time there was no escape. Immediately after his arrest he was taken to the central jail in Thiruvananthapuram, where he, aged 41, died within three months, even before his case was brought to trial.

Kochunni Plays a Trick

Banditry was as much a sport as an occupation for Kochunni, a pleasurable activity in itself. He loved to meet challenges head on, often without any thought of gain. Proving himself, his ingenuity, was reward enough for him.

This was the case with the trick he once played on a rich Nair in his home town. When the Nair built a new house for himself, he took every precaution to make it impregnable, and had its stone walls reinforced with wooden panels on the inside. Seeing this, a friend asked him: 'Walls are built either with wood or stone—why do you have both?'

'I've done this with Kochunni in mind,' said the Nair. 'The double wall would make it impossible for him to break in.'

Kochunni heard about the boast, and decided to teach the Nair a lesson. But he knew that it would be impossible for him to break into the house, and that he had to use some clever ruse to get at the valuables kept in the house. Then one day he came to know that the Nair had given a neighbour, one Krishna-pilla, a loan of one thousand rupees against the security of gold jewellery. This gave Kochunni an opening to trick the Nair.

As was his custom, he first went to the Nair and asked for a loan.

'I need a hundred rupees for an urgent expense,' he said.

'Alright,' said the Nair. 'I'll give you the money. But don't think I'm doing so out of fear. No one can break into this house, that's how strong I've built it.'

'So I've heard,' said Kochunni.

'Don't try anything rash,' warned the Nair, giving him the money.

Receiving the money from the Nair put Kochunni in a dilemma, as it was against his principles to rob anyone who helped him. On the other hand, he could not possibly ignore the challenge the Nair had thrown at him. So he contrived a stratagem to satisfy both these contrary impulses.

Now, the Nair was in the habit of taking an oil bath on Saturday evenings, an unfailing weekly ritual, rubbing his body thoroughly with sesame oil at home and going to the nearby river to bathe. But one Saturday some weeks after his exchange with Kochunni, his wife heard him return and call out to her soon after leaving the house to go to the river. This surprised her, for he usually spent a long time over the bath.

'You haven't bathed?' she asked, seeing him standing in the dusk near the veranda.

'No. On the way I saw Krishna-pilla coming to take back his jewels. Here's the money he borrowed,' he said, giving her a large cloth purse. 'I'm all covered with oil, so put this in the chest and bring his jewels.'

She did as she was told, and he left with the packet of jewels. This was Kochunni in disguise.

A few days later, Krishna-pilla came to the Nair's house to return the money he had borrowed. When the Nair opened the chest to take out Krishna-pilla's jewels, he found a large

cloth purse in it, and wondered how it got into the chest without his knowledge.

'What's this!' his wife laughed when he asked her about it. 'You gave it to me to keep in the chest. Don't you remember?'

'When?'

'Maybe ten-fifteen days back,' she said. 'It was a day you had gone to take an oil bath.'

'No,' said the Nair firmly. 'I did not give you this purse.'

'Yes, you did,' she said. 'You said it was the money that Krishna-pilla repaid, and you asked me to keep it in the chest and give you his jewels. Why are you so forgetful these days?'

'Are you crazy!' the Nair shouted. 'I know women are chronic liars, but this is too much.'

'You're the one that's crazy,' she said heatedly. 'I'm telling the truth.'

'Let's see what's in it anyway,' said the Nair and opened the purse, and was shocked to find it filled with blue-metal chips. He then realized that Kochunni had played a trick on his wife. He however said nothing about Kochunni to her, but went and told Krishna-pilla that he had somehow lost his jewels, and asked him how he should settle the matter.

'You decide,' said Krishna-pilla.

'I can either pay you the value of the lost jewels, or get new jewels made.'

'No need to make new jewels,' said Krishna-pilla. 'You can give me their value.'

'What would be their value?'

'When I brought it here, you estimated their value to be two thousand rupees,' said Krishna-pilla. 'You need to pay me only that. I'm not avaricious.'

'Fine,' said the Nair. 'But I don't have two thousand rupees with me just now. I'll give you a thousand rupees now. The balance I'll pay you within a week, and for that I'll give you a promissory note.'

'No need for a promissory note,' said Krishna-pilla. 'Your word is enough.'

But the Nair insisted on giving him the promissory note.

'We should never be casual in money matters,' he said, handing over the note. 'But I've one request. You shouldn't tell anyone about this incident. I don't mind losing money, but I don't like to lose face.'

'No one will hear about it from me,' assured Krishna-pilla.

In a while Kochunni came there. 'Why are you both looking so glum?' he asked, seeing the Nair and his wife sitting dejectedly in the veranda.

Immediately the Nair's wife, much to the annoyance of her husband and ignoring his signals to caution her, told Kochunni how some thief had tricked them.

'What a shame!' said Kochunni in mock sympathy. 'It does seem that strong walls are no protection against a clever thief, doesn't it?'

He then held out a bundle to the Nair. 'Here are Krishna-pilla's jewels,' he said. 'Take it to him and collect your money and promissory note. I don't want anything from this. But one thing: please don't boast hereafter about thwarting Kochunni.'

∽

Revenge of an Elephant

In medieval and early modern times, it was a matter of prestige for affluent temples and aristocratic families in Kerala to own an elephant or two. The animal was invariably treated with great affection, like a member of the family, and there was usually something of a filial bond between elephants and their mahouts. But the high risk of their profession sometimes turned mahouts into drunkards, who ill-treated and exploited the animals. And often they had to pay with their lives for such misdeeds. The elephant, as the saying goes, never forgets.

Such is the love-hate story of Neelakantan, a legendary late nineteenth century elephant of the Shiva temple at Panthalam in south Kerala, and his mahouts. The temple had bought him as a baby from itinerant Arab merchants. The frisky little fellow soon became the pet of the local people, and they pampered him by regularly feeding him with plantain, jaggery, shelled coconut and other delicacies. Under such loving care Neelakantan grew into robust adulthood, a magnificent elephant with a proud and intelligent bearing. His only flaw was that he had virtually no tusks, and had to be fitted with an artificial pair, initially of silver—which he did not like and broke off—and then of wood painted to look like ivory.

Soon after he was bought, Neelakantan was put in the charge of two mahouts, Madhavan and Govindan. They were brothers, but entirely unlike each other in character. Madhavan loved Neelakantan like his own child, called him makan (son), and shared with him all he ate and drank, including toddy and arrack, and never beat him or even scolded him. Nor did he ever overwork or exploit him for personal gain. Neelakantan reciprocated the love, and cared for Madhavan as much as a fond son would care for his father, even carrying him home by picking him up gently with his trunk on the occasions when he got drunk and fell on the way.

But the nature of the relationship between Govindan and Neelakantan was quite different. Govindan was a slave-driver, and his only interest in Neelakantan was to make him work without the knowledge of the temple authorities and pocket the earnings. The elephant resented this and was slack in performing tasks for Govindan, and was therefore quite often beaten by the mahout. Neelakantan bided his time to take revenge. One day Govindan took the elephant to pull out a huge log from the nearby river and drag it to a house some distance away. Neelakantan could pull the log out of the water, but found it hard to drag it through the soft soil of the river bank. So, after pulling it a short distance, he dropped it and stood aside. At this, Govindan, who had taken a substantial advance for the job, struck Neelakantan hard on a vital spot. That, on top of all the beatings he had received over the years, finally broke Neelakantan's forbearance. Enraged, he shook his head violently to fling Govindan from his neck to the ground, and trampled him to death in a flash of fury. Then, trumpeting loudly, as elephants do when they kill, Neelakantan ran about madly, terrifying and scattering everyone.

When Madhavan heard about the incident, he immediately rushed to subdue Neelakantan. Though people tried to hold him back, warning him that it would be suicidal to approach the maddened elephant, Madhavan boldly went up to him and took hold of him by the ear, as one would do to a mischievous child. Neelakantan immediately calmed down and, on the order of the mahout, penitently followed him, and allowed himself to be chained. People were amazed by this instantaneous change of the elephant's mood, but their old admiration for him was now tinged with fear. Neelakantan had become a killer.

And he would kill again and again. But only when provoked beyond endurance. And his victims were all vicious mahouts. Otherwise Neelakantan never hurt anyone. And he always remained affectionate towards those who cared for him. Thus when his favourite mahout, Madhavan, died of smallpox, he was so disconsolate that for seven days he did not touch food or water. He was especially fond of children, who could play with him without fear of harm. Once, when he was rampaging in musth, he came across a group of children playing under a mango tree. They scattered at his menacing approach, but one little girl fell in a dead faint. Seeing this, Neelakantan lifted her with his trunk and laid her on the veranda of a nearby house, before running off again.

❧

Sabarimala Ayyappan

The medieval kingdom of Pantalam in southern Kerala is believed to have been founded in the twelfth century by a branch of the Pandya royal family of Madura in Tamil Nadu. It was a tiny state consisting of just a few villages, but it endured for some six hundred years, till the late eighteenth century, when Travancore absorbed it, because the Pantalam raja, who had hypothecated his lands to the king of Travancore for two hundred and twenty thousand rupees, was unable to redeem the pledge.

The family deity of the Pantalam rajas was Sabarimala Sastha (Ayyappan), and it was their custom over the generations to go on pilgrimage to Sabarimala every year for the Makara Sankranthi festival in January. But this practice was neglected by one of the rajas, because the journey to the shrine—in the deep jungle some fifty kilometres east of Pantalam—was arduous and took many days. Besides, the raja could not bear to be separated even for a few days from his beloved wife, a princess of the neighbouring Kayamkulam kingdom. He was so obsessed with her that he took to living with her in the Kayamkulam palace, and for some twelve years he did not go to Sabarimala, or even visit his own kingdom.

Then one night the raja had a terrible nightmare, and began screaming, 'Ayyo-ayyo tiger! Ayyo-ayyo bear!' When his frightened wife shook him awake and asked what the matter was, he said, 'It's nothing, just a nightmare,' and went back to sleep. But the next night he again had the same nightmare, and this then became a regular nightly occurrence. Later he came to have the nightmare several times every night, so hardly anyone in the palace could sleep because of his hollering and shrieking. Physicians and exorcists were then called in to treat him, but his condition only grew worse day by day. So one morning the Kayamkulam raja took him aside and said to him, 'Look, no one here is able to sleep because of your nightmares. So I think it's best that you should now go back to your own kingdom, and return only after you have got over this madness.'

The Pantalam raja felt humiliated by these words, but more than that he was distressed that he would be separated from his wife. But that night, in addition to the usual nightmare, he had a dream in which he heard someone tell him, 'It's now twelve years since you worshipped at Sabarimala. If you now go and worship Ayyappan for twelve days, and thereafter regularly perform the monthly puja there, you will be cured. As for the Kayamkulam raja, he will suffer for insulting you.'

Believing that it was Ayyappan himself who appeared in his dream and gave him the advice, the raja decided to obey and, taking leave of his wife, he set out for Pantalam the very next day. As soon as he returned to Pantalam, his nightmares ceased altogether. He then went on a pilgrimage to Sabarimala, performed the twelve-day puja there, and presented to the idol a gold crown and a pearl necklace. And that entirely cured him of his madness.

But from the day the Pantalam raja left, the Kayamkulam raja began to show signs of madness. He would not bathe or even eat, unless someone forced him to do so. And if anyone asked him anything, whatever the question, all he would say was, 'The bear has littered! The tiger has littered!' A famous augur was then called in, and he ascertained that the illness was caused by the displeasure of Ayyappan for ill-treating the Pantalam raja, and that the remedy would be to make a propitiatory offering at Sabarimala. When this was done, the raja recovered.

Presently the Pantalam raja returned to Kayamkulam. But he found it difficult to go to Sabarimala every month. When he was worrying about this, he had a dream one night in which he heard the deity tell him, 'It is not necessary for you to come every month to Sabarimala. I will come to a place near you. In a few days the Kayamkulam raja would be holding his annual contest in martial skills. I will come there to participate in it, and where the arrow I shoot falls, there you will find my idol.'

On the day of the contest a divinely handsome youth presented himself to the Kayamkulam raja.

'Who are you?' the raja asked.

'I'm a Malayali,' the youth said.

'Where do you live?'

'In a hill to the east.'

'And your name?'

'Ayyappan.'

'Why have you come?'

'To participate in the contest.'

'What's your weapon?'

'I'm proficient in the use of most weapons.'

'Alright,' said the raja. 'You can join the contest.'

The youth easily won in all the events, and when the raja asked him what reward he wanted, he requested for a stretch of land to be given to him tax free, at the place where his arrow shot fell. The raja agreed to this. The youth then shot an arrow, and himself led the royal officers and the Pantalam raja to the place where it fell, and then disappeared.

The arrow was found in an island in the lagoon some distance to the south-east of Kayamkulam, and there the raja found a stone idol of Ayyappan, and on it were the gold crown and pearl necklace that he had donated at Sabarimala. Hearing about the miraculous appearance of the idol, the Kayamkulam raja built an Ayyappan temple there, and also a palace for the Pantalam raja. And this enabled the raja to perform his devotions to Ayyappan without leaving his wife even for a day.

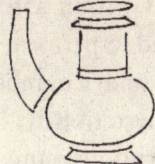

Gods do not die, but they do sometimes fade away, as it happened even to chief Vedic gods like Indra and Varuna. And in Kerala several local deities popular in medieval times have long left the scene. One such god was Karuppuswamy, a forest deity associated with the Sastha, for whom there is a shrine close to the Achankoil Sastha temple near Kollam.

Karuppuswamy was at one time an important deity in south Kerala, and it was common for the affluent of the region to offer him a sacrifice called Karuppanoottu, for the fulfilment of their desires. It was not, however, necessary to go to his temple to perform this rite, for the chief priest of the temple would perform it at any place of the donor's choice. Karuppanoottu was an expensive ritual, for large quantities of rice, coconuts, arrack, cannabis, opium, betel leaves, and very many other provisions were required for its performance. Fire-walking too was part of the rite.

Among those who traditionally conducted the Karuppanoottu ritual once a year was the forest department of the Travancore government. But when a British officer assumed charge of the department he gave up the practice.

And it so happened that in the year the sacrifice was not performed, hardly any wild elephants were caught in the traps set by the government. The local people then told the officer that this was because of the displeasure of Karuppuswamy.

'Alright,' the officer said. 'We'll make the offering if elephants now fall in the pits.' To his surprise, several elephants were captured within a few days of making the promise. Still he neglected to perform the promised rites, and in consequence (so it was said) a number of the newly captured elephants began to die mysteriously. His staff then reminded him of his offer to Karuppuswamy, and he, though still sceptical, agreed to perform the rites.

A large shed was erected near the forest office, and a messenger sent to invite the priest of the Karuppuswamy shrine to perform the rite. The officer then made all the arrangements for the ritual, but he also took certain secret measures to test the genuineness of the miraculous potencies claimed for the rite. The arrack required for the rite, for instance, was buried in sealed jars in the ground, and the pit for fire-walking was made very large and deep, and several heavy iron chains were placed in it, between the layers of smouldering coal.

When the priest arrived at the site, he was taken aback by the enormous size of the fire-pit. But he said nothing, and left it to his deity to save his honour. He then took a ritual bath, wore a fresh dhoti, took in his hand some sandalwood paste, flowers and water, and stood facing the east for a while in silent prayer, his eyes closed. Then he began the rituals. A conch was blown, and pipes and drums started up. Soon a large number of people gathered there to witness the ceremony, and they rent the air with their yodels and the chant 'Saranam-Ayyappa!' Presently the British officer arrived there on a horse, and took his seat in a chair close to the shed, nonchalantly twirling the horsewhip.

As the rites proceeded, the demeanour and the very appearance of the priest changed into something out of the world, and he began to writhe convulsively, as if possessed by Karuppuswamy's spirit. He then turned to the officer and asked, in a voice that seemed to come from some deep cave: 'So you want to test me?' The officer merely smirked, viewing all this as a charade.

'Watch,' said the priest.

He then went and stood where the officer had secretly buried the jars of arrack, flung a fistful of ash over the place and roared once defiantly. Immediately the earth over the jars fissured and opened up, the lids of the jars flew open, and the arrack in them began to burn like fireworks, shooting skyward. As the aghast officer looked on numbly, the priest snatched the whip from him, leapt on his horse, and rode it into the fire-pit and made it prance on the burning coals for a while. He then dismounted and took the horse to the officer, and on examination it was found that the coals had not singed even a hair on its legs.

Then again the frenzied priest leapt into the fire-pit, took a couple of red-hot chains from it, wound one of them around his torso, and carried the other chain in his hand and gave it to the officer. The officer, as if in a trance himself, took it, but in his hands it felt cool and light. The priest then asked him to put the chain down and pick it up again, but when he bent down to take it, he found it glowing red-hot, and shrank back.

'So?' asked the priest. 'Are the tests over? Or do you wish to try me again?'

'Enough,' said the alarmed officer. 'Please forgive my

offence. Hereafter the ritual will be done every year at government expense, and not only that, I'll have one performed at my own expense too.'

'Good,' said the priest. 'I've no resentment towards you.'

Trial by Terror

The kingdoms of Kerala were all tiny in the late medieval period, and the power and resources of their rulers limited. And they and their subjects lived, as it were, within sight of each other. In that environment there was little scope for royal tyranny, and the rajas were generally mild-mannered and benevolent. Sakthan Thamburan, the late eighteenth century ruler of Kochi, was an exception to this. Though an able administrator, he was pitiless in crushing the wealth and power of the old landed aristocracy in the kingdom, and his manner of enforcing law and order was hardly lawful.

Sakthan was born on Thursday, tenth Karkadakam (July–August) 1751, a new-moon day. Astrologically, the time of his birth was considered inauspicious, so his distraught mother approached a sanyasi in a nearby temple to seek remedial measures. He sent her some sanctified flowers, saying that the evil consequences of the stellar configuration would be removed if those flowers were scattered under the bed of the baby. This consoled the parents, but the misfortune that was diverted from the prince fell on the hapless people of the kingdom.

An intelligent and active child, the prince was particularly proficient in the martial arts, and was noted for his valour and ferocity even as a boy. This earned him the nickname Sakthan (Mighty), and it was by this name that he would be known in history. The first known demonstration of his particular brand of mightiness was given when he, as prince, was asked by the reigning raja to deal with a case of highway robbery. The crime was committed by some Mapillas (Christians) against a Namboodiri when he was going from Tripunittura (the seat of the royal court) to the nearby town of Ernakulam. On the complaint of the Namboodiri, the raja asked the prince to go and live in Ernakulam for some time and take measures to ensure that similar incidents did not take place in future.

The day after he moved into Ernakulam, the prince issued an order summoning all the Mapillas living in that area to assemble the next morning on the bank of the lagoon there, each with a large pot and a couple of yards of rope. Some five hundred Mapillas assembled in obedience to the order, and the prince went to them with a contingent of soldiers. 'You must tell me who among you waylaid the Namboodiri a few days back,' he said to them. 'If the guilty confess, I would be lenient in punishing them, and the rest of you can go in peace. But if the guilty are not found, all of you will be punished most grievously.'

There was no response from the Mapillas, who probably thought that the prince was bluffing. But to their horror he had a number of them seized at random and taken in boats and drowned in the deepest part of the lagoon, by tying to their necks the pots they had brought with them. He then ordered that the remaining Mapillas should assemble at the same spot the next morning, and left the place.

The terrified Mapilla leaders then collected a good amount

of money from among themselves and went to see the prince. They told him that they did not know who the guilty were, and requested him to accept the purse in atonement of what some reckless members of the community had done. They further guaranteed, against the security of their own lives, that no member of their community would thereafter commit any such offence.

'I accept your pledge,' said the prince. 'You may go now, but don't forget what would happen if your assurance fails.'

The prince then returned to Tripunittura and presented the purse to the raja saying that it was the offering made by the Mapillas of Ernakulam to compensate the Namboodiri, and the raja in turn handed it over to the Namboodiri, who was overjoyed that what he got now was far more than what he had lost.

Sakthan Thamburan was ruthless and arbitrary, and he had a demonic temper, but unlike most other tyrants, he was not a sexual predator. In fact, he was rather continent, and thought of getting married only when he was past thirty. He then took a woman from Thrissur as his wife. But he was not blessed with marital happiness, for his wife turned out to be a faithless woman. Soon after he married her, the prince had appointed one Kunjitti Menon, a childhood friend and trusted officer, to assist her in household management, but Kunjitti apparently transgressed propriety in his dealings with her. The prince solved the problem in his characteristic manner.

'You seem to be avoiding me these days,' said the prince to Kunjitti one day. 'It is as if your desire is to see the last of me. My desire, on the other hand, is to see you always. So I've devised a means to satisfy both our desires.'

As Kunjitti tensed, the prince called out, 'Who's there!'

Immediately two soldiers presented themselves, and the

prince ordered: 'Take Kunjitti out and tear out his eyes and place them before me. Right away!'

Kunjitti pleaded with the prince to spare him, offering various explanations and apologies, but to no avail.

When the raja heard of the blinding, he called Kunjitti to him and said, 'I'm so sorry to hear that the prince has committed this outrage. Tell me, what can I do to compensate you? Whatever you wish, I'll arrange for it.'

'If you've compassion for me, please take my life immediately,' said Kunjitti. 'That's my only desire.'

The raja took him at his word, and had him executed immediately.

❧

Fatal Obsession

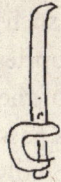

Sakthan Thamburan was a loner, who often toured his kingdom alone and incognito, travelling on foot, carrying a cloth bundle tied to a staff, and armed only with a sword concealed in the staff. He carried provisions and cooking vessels in the bundle, and often cooked his own food during his travels. Totally unpredictable, he was an enigma even to his closest courtiers. And he never allowed anyone to influence his decisions or take advantage of his favour. This was a lesson that one of his captains learned too late to save his own life.

Soon after his accession to the throne in 1790, the raja introduced a number of administrative reforms for the security of the kingdom and the enforcement of law and order, and built new forts in Tripunittura and Thrissur, the two towns where he mainly resided. In Thrissur, the guard duty of the outer walls of the fort was assigned to Thiyya soldiers, over whom he appointed a captain of their own caste.

This captain, titled Thandan, was a favourite of the raja. But that did not save him when he transgressed caste propriety and propositioned a Nair woman, whom he had happened to see one morning at the Vadakkunathan temple, where she had gone for ritual ablutions and prayers, as was the custom of the Nair women who lived in the vicinity of the temple. The moment Thandan saw her, very beautiful and in the full bloom of youth, he became utterly infatuated with her, and began to hound her during her daily visits to the temple.

The woman paid no attention whatever to him, but the desire to possess her became such an obsession with him that he lost all sense of social propriety. And, instead of holding himself in restraint because of the responsible office he held, he sought to consummate his passion by misusing his power, and one day spoke to her boldly and insistently about his passion.

This greatly perturbed the woman. She was afraid to spurn Thandan, knowing his closeness to the raja. On the other hand, her sense of honour would not let her yield to him. For some days she managed to put him off with some excuse or other, but this only further inflamed his passion. And one day, when he saw her going into the royal fort for some work, he decided to bring the matter to a head. 'How long are you going to evade me with excuses?' he asked. 'This cannot go on. Don't you play with me! You know the raja is in my hands. So take care. You must give me an answer today, when you return from the fort. Think well of what the consequences will be if you reject me.'

She made no answer, but realized that she could not put him off with excuses any more. Her only hope was to appeal to the raja to save her honour, though she was doubtful whether he would favour her, considering that Thandan was close to him. But as there was no other way out for her, she decided to seek the raja's protection. 'Whatever happens thereafter, that I'll have to accept as my fate,' she decided.

The raja was at this time residing in Thrissur. So she went

and stood suppliantly in the front courtyard of the royal residence. When the raja saw her standing there, he sent a servant to find out what she wanted. 'I've a complaint to place before Thirumeni,' she said.

The raja then called her to him and asked, 'What's your grievance?'

When she told him of being harassed by Thandan, the raja, as she feared, said, 'If he has such a passion, it would be good to gratify him. Why not?'

'This is most distressing to me,' she made bold to tell him.

'What's there to be distressed about?' said the raja. 'It's a simple matter. You must let him come to you today itself—ask him to come at four hours after sunset, when people are not likely to see him visiting you. This is my decision. You may go now.'

She had no alternative but to obey the royal order. At the gate of the fort, Thandan was waiting for her. 'So what have you decided?' he asked. 'You must give me a firm answer right now.' And she, as advised by the raja, told him to visit her that night at the specified time. Thandan was ecstatic to hear her words, and he spent the rest of the day cursing the interminable time it was taking for the sun to set.

Meanwhile the raja summoned his military commander and asked him to take a large vessel of oil and a good length of gauze, and station himself with a few soldiers and drummers at a particular place after sunset. 'We will have some fun tonight,' he said. After supper he himself, with a couple of guards, went and hid near the woman's house.

Thandan arrived at the woman's house at the appointed time, wearing fine clothes and a garland of fragrant flowers, and his body perfumed with attar, rosewater, sandalwood paste and musk. But as he was about to step into the house, the raja, who had sneaked up behind him, seized him by his chignon and flung him back, hissing, 'Not that way! This way!'

As Thandan fell, the raja held him down with his foot and called out to the soldiers to bind his body with the cloth they had brought and drench him with oil. 'Now set fire to him,' he ordered. 'Let the drums be beaten to drown his screams.'

It was quite a fiery climax to Thandan's flaming passion.

Sakthan's Revenge

Sakthan Thamburan was given to volcanic eruptions of temper, even over trivial matters. Once he very nearly beheaded a palace official for plucking a few leaves from one of the pipal saplings he had planted along the royal avenue in Tripunittura and had expressly declared as protected trees. The official thought nothing of what he did, as it was a matter of just a few leaves, and he had plucked them only to feed the pet goats of a prince. But the moment Sakthan heard of the incident, he flew into a rage, summoned the official and drew his sword to slay him. The man was saved only because the prince, the owner of the pet goats, rushed in and clung to the raja saying, 'Kill me first before killing him.' The raja then flung away his sword in disgust, cursing the mildness of the prince.

Not so lucky was Devaresan, a Konkani merchant of Kochi, who inadvertently offended the raja by delivering late, by an hour or so, a quantity of sugar that the raja had one day ordered for a palace function. The occasion was the grand feast that the raja held in Ernakulam as part of the first death anniversary ceremonies of his aunt, his mother's younger sister, who had brought him up after his mother died during his infancy. Though everything at the feast went off well, some Brahmin invitees grumbled that the sugar was served late.

To sweeten the tongues of his guests, the raja then heaped on them generous gifts, far more than usual, so they presently changed their tune and praised the magnificence of the feast. But the humiliation of the delayed serving of the sugar rankled in the raja's mind. So, after all the guests had departed, he called the commander of his army and said to him: 'Devaresan is treating us casually because he is living under the protection of the Dutch in the Kochi fort. This cannot be tolerated. Tomorrow morning when I wake up, the first thing I see should be his severed head.'

The captain immediately set out for Kochi in a boat, armed with a belt-sword and carrying a large purse of money. The Kochi fort was originally built by the Portuguese but was at this time under the Dutch. The captain entered the fort before its gates closed at ten in the night and went straight to the office of Devaresan. When the captain arrived, the merchant was at his desk, checking the day's accounts. He received the captain courteously and enquired about the reason for the sudden visit.

'Is there anything urgently required?' he asked.

'Yes,' said the captain. 'We need some lengths of silk urgently.'

'For this you need not have troubled yourself to come,' said Devaresan. 'If you had sent a messenger I would have brought the cloth to you.'

'You know the raja—he wants everything to be done instantly,' said the captain. 'He asked me to do this myself, to make sure that his orders are executed exactly. Let's have a look at what you have.'

'Ordinary silks are kept here on the ground floor,' said Devaresan. 'Fine silks are on the first floor. What is it that you require?'

'We need some of both,' said the captain.

Devaresan then measured out the required quantity of ordinary silk and gave it to the captain, and then took him upstairs to show him the fine silks. After completing the transaction, they sat for a long time chatting, as the fort gates had by then closed and the captain could leave the place only when they opened again at 4 a.m.

'Is the raja angry with me for the delay in supplying the sugar?' asked Devaresan. 'There was a lot of confusion that day, and in the midst of it I forgot about the sugar. As soon as I remembered I sent it.'

'That's nothing,' said the captain. 'The raja might be a little displeased, but he'll forget it if you will call on him and apologize.'

'Had I been living in an area under the raja's control, he would have had me executed by now,' the merchant remarked. He was the head of the Konkani merchants of the region and was rich and powerful, and there was a hint of insolence in his words. 'I'm safe only because I live in this fort.'

'Forget the incident,' said the captain, lulling the merchant's anxiety. But a little later, he quietly pulled out his belt-sword and swiftly severed Devaresan's head before he could shout for help. He then rolled the head in silk, stepped past the slumbering servants on the ground floor, and went and hid near the fort gate. As soon as the gate opened, he got out, and sped in his boat to Ernakulam. There he hung the merchant's head at the door of the royal bedchamber and waited for the raja to wake up.

The raja was delighted to see the merchant's head hanging

from the lintel of his door as he opened it in the morning. 'You've done a heroic deed,' he said, congratulating the captain.

'It's not my heroism, but the irresistible force of your command that accomplished this,' said the captain modestly.

The Sorcerer Padre

Achristian priest as a sorcerer? Such was the strange
fusion of vocations in Katamattath Kathanar, a
renowned occultist of late-medieval Kerala. His real name
was Paulose, and he was a poor orphan boy brought up and
educated by a kindly parish priest. When he was serving as a
deacon under the priest, he one day got lost in the nearby
forest where he had gone to look for some cattle of the priest
that had wandered off. A search was mounted for him the
next day, but when no trace of him was found, it was feared
that he had fallen prey to some wild beast.

But Paulose was only lost, not dead. He had taken the
wrong turn while returning from the woods, and at nightfall
found himself at the mouth of a cave deep in the forest. There
he was caught by some wild men and taken inside the cave
to their chief. Though the opening of the cave was narrow
and dark, it was spacious inside and well lit with lamps. The
chief sat in a high chair, and around him stood several men
in humble postures, as before a king. All were stark naked.

The cave was apparently the secret retreat of some occult
sect, which did not take kindly to intruders. Their chief

however took a liking for Paulose, and said to him, 'You seem to be a decent young man. If you are willing to live here according to our rules, you can stay with us, and we will meet all you needs. But you will not be allowed to leave this place alive.'

Paulose had no alternative but to agree, and he spent some twelve years there as a disciple of the chief, from whom he learned sorcery and various magical skills. But gradually the desire to return to his own people grew strong in him, though he was also reluctant to betray the trust that the chief had reposed in him. As he grew wan and depressed because of these contrary pressures, the chief one day asked him, 'What's troubling you? You want to go home?'

'Yes sire,' Paulose said truthfully. 'At the same time I don't like to leave you. I certainly don't want to leave without your blessing.'

'I'm pleased with your honesty,' said the chief. 'I can't give you permission to leave—that is against our rules. But if you can get past the guards somehow, you may go. I'll pretend that I didn't know anything about it.'

Paulose escaped from the cave that very night by casting a spell on the guards, and set out for home. On the way, weary and hungry, he stopped at the hut of a poor old woman and asked for some rice gruel.

'I'm sorry, my son,' the woman said. 'There is nothing to eat here. I didn't cook today, as there was no rice.'

'See whether you have at least a grain of rice somewhere,' Paulose pleaded.

'What good would that do?' the woman asked.

'Bring it,' said Paulose. 'Then we'll see.'

She then scoured in her rice basket and brought him a grain of broken rice.

'This will do,' said Paulose. 'Now hurry up and boil water to cook rice.'

The woman thought that the man was crazy, but there was a certain air about him that made her obey. When the water boiled, Paulose muttered a mantra over the grain of rice and put it in the water, and presently, to the astonishment of the woman, the pot boiled over with cooked rice.

This was the first miracle that Paulose performed after leaving the cave. He then returned home, where the priest received him with great joy. A couple of years later he was ordained as a priest, and was thereafter known as Katamattath Kathanar. His reputation as a miracle worker spread rapidly, and it came to be believed that there was no occult feat that was beyond his power to accomplish.

There was only one other sorcerer in Kerala at this time to rival the reputation of the Kathanar, one Kunjamun Potti. Potti was proud that he had at his command several genii, and that the Kathanar had none, while the Kathanar was proud of having superior magical skills. They had a chance to test each other once, when the Kathanar visited Potti on his invitation.

Knowing that Potti usually travelled in a boat rowed by invisible genii, the Kathanar arrived at Potti's place in a boat without any boatmen.

'Where are the boatmen?' asked Potti.

'I couldn't find any boatmen, so I just got in and told the boat to bring me here,' said the Kathanar disarmingly.

Potti realized that the Kathanar was flaunting his magical power, but he said nothing, and showed him all the hospitality due to a guest. They had a meal together, and afterwards sat talking for a long while, exchanging anecdotes. And when the Kathanar took his leave, Potti accompanied him to the jetty. But the Kathanar could not find his boat there, and on looking around, saw it atop a huge mango tree. The Kathanar knew that Potti had got this done by his genii to show off in turn, and he said, 'I had left my boat at your jetty. It's your responsibility to get it down.'

'How can I bring down the boat from the tree?' Potti protested innocently. 'If you have the power, bring it down yourself.'

'I know what you're up to,' said the Kathanar good-humouredly. 'If you won't have it brought down, I'll get your women to come naked out of your house and climb the tree—isn't it better to avoid that?'

'You can do that?' challenged Potti. 'Alright then, try.'

'Look,' said Kathanar. As Potti turned around, he saw to his horror his women coming out of the house naked!

'Ayyayyo, please don't humiliate me,' pleaded Potti. 'Send them back, and I'll have your boat brought down.'

They then took an oath never again to compete with each other, and parted as friends.

❦

Death Reader

Thaikatt Paramesvaran Moossad, a nineteenth century descendant of one of the eight traditional families of Namboodiri physicians of Kerala, was a great healer, but more than that he was renowned for his paranormal power to detect the signs of death in people, irrespective of their outward appearance and apparent state of health. It was as if he could see the life-force in a man burning like a flame within his body, shining bright or fading.

Once when he was on his way to some place, he saw three condemned criminals being taken in a procession by soldiers to be hanged. The prisoners were wearing flower garlands and were led by a band of drummers, as was the custom in Kerala those days. Seeing this, Moossad called out to the officer in charge of the military detail escorting the prisoners, and, pointing to one of the prisoners, told him, 'That man is not to be executed.' The officer did not understand the significance of what Moossad said, and in any case he could not but carry out the royal order. So he ignored Moossad and proceeded with the preparations to execute the convicts.

The gallows were set up on a river bank, and when the procession reached there, the officer asked the prisoners whether they had any last wish. Two of them said that they had none, but the man identified by Moossad said that he would like to pluck a tender coconut from a tree on the river bank and drink its water before being hanged. The officer saw no harm in letting him do that. It was not a difficult tree to climb, as it was leaning low over the river. The condemned man easily got to its top, plucked a coconut, cut off its top with a knife and, sitting there, drank the sweet water in the shell. Then he began to climb down slowly, but about halfway down he leapt from the tree into the river and swam away to freedom.

When the officer reported the matter to the raja, he also mentioned what Moossad had told him on the way. So the raja summoned Moossad and asked him why he had said that the man was not to be executed.

'I didn't see any signs of death on him,' said Moossad. 'So I felt that there was no point in taking him for execution.'

'You can foresee death?'

'Yes.'

'Alright,' said the raja. 'Can you tell me when I'll die?'

'I can,' said Moossad. 'But why do you want to know that?'

'If I know when I'll die, then I can perform some good deeds for the benefit of my soul.'

'Good deeds can be done at any time,' said Moossad. 'You don't have to know the time of your death for that.'

'Still . . . ?'

'You will die the day after I come here next,' was all that Moossad would say.

It was many months later, during the birthday celebrations of the raja, that Moossad next visited the palace. He arrived the night before the birthday, but went to see the raja only the next day. The raja was just then sitting down to the birthday feast, but as he began eating, he felt uneasy, saying, 'My head is spinning.' Seeing this Moossad rushed to the attending princes and warned them about the impending death of the raja, and told them to immediately lay him on the floor on a bed of sand and grass, as custom prescribed. In a short time, as Moossad had foreseen, the raja passed away.

Similarly, another day when he was in a temple he saw a Namboodiri peacefully slumbering in the bath-house there, and saw the signs of death on him, though he was not known to be suffering from any ailment. Moossad asked the man's friends to wake him up and take him home at once. The man died soon after reaching home.

Because of his reputation of being able to foresee death, if Moossad did not prescribe any treatment to a patient, it was invariably assumed that the case was hopeless. This was what happened in the case of a Namboodiri who consulted him for the treatment of an itchy eruption on his skin.

'Don't think that this is an ordinary itch,' said Moossad on examining the patient. 'It will gradually spread all over the body, and could prove fatal.'

He prescribed no medicine, and this threw the Namboodiri into deep depression, fearing that his death was imminent. People commiserated with him, but all were of the opinion that if Moossad said that the case was hopeless, then there was nothing that anyone could do about it. But one of his friends disagreed with this. 'Moossad may be right, and maybe no man can cure you,' he said. 'But god can. If you worship the sun god, I think you'll be cured.'

No harm in trying that, thought the Namboodiri, and the very next day he began a rigorous ritual of sun worship, sitting in the sun facing the east from dawn to noon, and then turning around to face the west till sunset. For forty-one days he did this without remission, and towards the end his entire body, over which the itch had spread, turned black like coal. Then his skin began to peel off. And that completely cured the Namboodiri.

He then went to see Moossad. And the physician said to him, 'I'm not god. I can cure only what can be cured by medicine. But god can cure even incurable diseases. Had I prescribed any medicine for you, you would not have turned to god, and you would have died. That's why I did not treat you.'

Elephant Thieves

The border between the kingdoms of Kochi and Travancore was not clearly demarcated in the eighteenth century, especially in the hill country. Therefore when Ramavarma Raja, the king of Travancore, was told that some of the elephant traps set up by Kochi extended into his territory, he ignored it, particularly because he had an excellent relationship with Sakthan Thamburan, the raja of Kochi. But when he learned that a young tusker of extraordinary grace and bearing, and having all the auspicious marks, had fallen into one of the pit-traps, he desired to obtain it for himself.

Meanwhile Sakthan Thamburan, on being told of the excellence of the tusker, himself arrived at the site to personally see to it that the beast was safely brought out of the pit and caged in an elephant pen. As this pen was well within the Kochi territory, it then became necessary for the Travancore raja to use some clever stratagem to seize the elephant without directly offending Sakthan. Luckily, there was a man in his service who was equal to this task—Kunjikutty, an officer of great physical prowess and exceptional skills, brilliant as a strategist and spy, and proficient in occult arts.

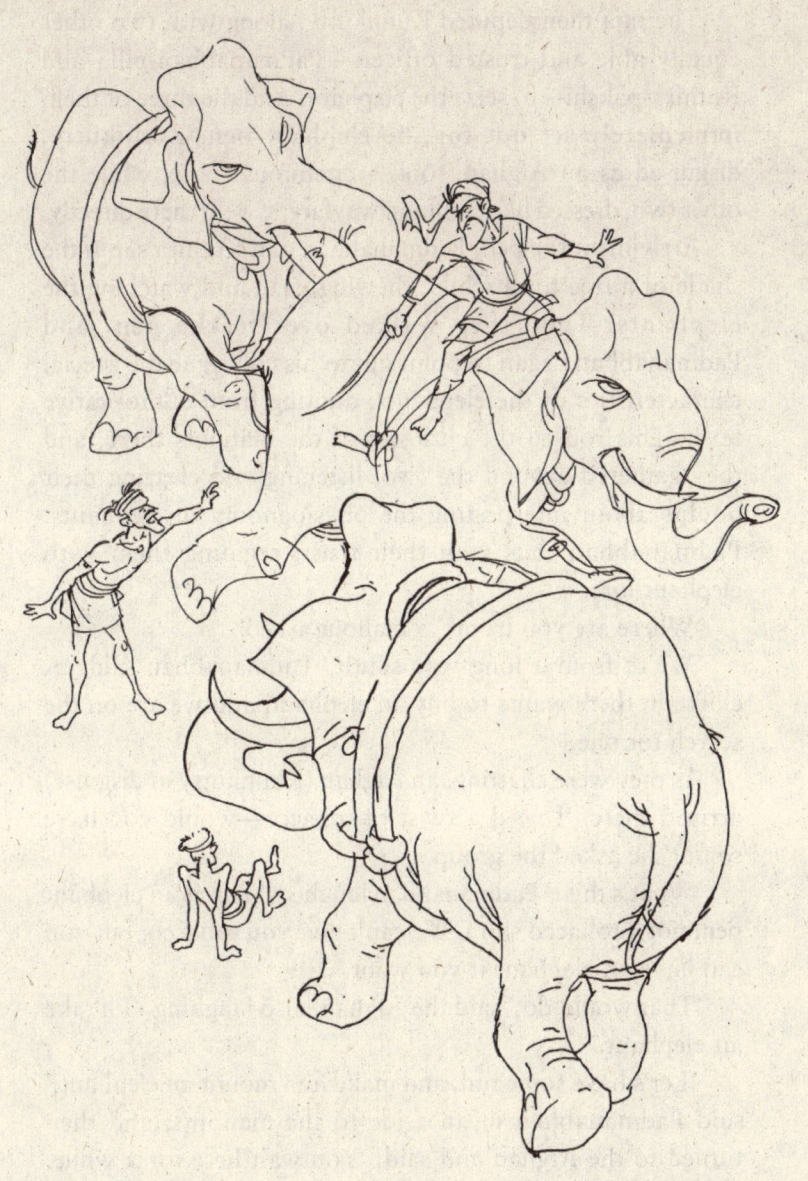

The raja then deputed Kunjikutty, along with two other equally able and trusted officers—Padmanabhan-pilla and Kuthira-pakshi—to seize the elephant. And the three of them immediately set out for the elephant pen. Kunjikutty, disguised as an Afghan, took a circuitous route, while the other two, dressed like common wayfarers, went there directly.

Arriving at the pen, Padmanabhan and Kuthira sat in the shade of a tree for a while, chewing paan and watching the elephants. Then they walked over to the pen, and Padmanabhan began to point out to his colleague the special characteristics of the elephants, quoting from authoritative texts. This roused the curiosity of the mahouts there, and they gathered around the two, listening and clearing their doubts about interpreting the physiognomy of elephants. Padmanabhan thus won their trust, regaling them with elephant lore.

'Where are you from?' a mahout asked.

'We're from a long way south,' Padmanabhan said. 'A chieftain there wants to buy an elephant, and we are on the search for one.'

As they were chatting, an Afghan (Kunjikutty in disguise) arrived there. 'I need a twist of tobacco—would you have some?' he asked the group.

'What's this?' Padmanabhan laughed. 'This is an elephant pen, not a tobacco shop. We can't give you tobacco, but you can have an elephant if you want.'

'That would do,' said the Afghan, also laughing. 'I'll take an elephant.'

'Let's have some fun, and make him mount an elephant,' said Padmanabhan in an aside to the mahouts, and then turned to the Afghan and said, 'You wait here for a while. We've to go some place now, but when we return we'll let you mount an elephant.'

Padmanabhan and Kuthira then took the mahouts to a nearby toddy shop and got them thoroughly drunk, though the two themselves remained absolutely sober.

'Which elephant would you like to mount?' Padmanabhan asked the Afghan when he returned with the tipsy mahouts.

'This one,' said the Afghan, pointing to the young tusker.

'You can't mount that one,' a mahout said. 'He has not yet been tamed. Besides, he is very ferocious, and just the other day had killed a mahout.'

'If he wants to risk his life, it's not our problem,' said Padmanabhan. They were all jolly friends now, and it was no great problem for Padmanabhan to persuade the soused mahouts to let the Afghan have his way. The tusker was then brought out of the pen, tied to two tame elephants on its flanks.

'If you're ready to die, he's all yours,' Padmanabhan said to the Afghan.

Instantly the Afghan leapt on to the back of the elephant. And, as the astounded mahouts stood agape, he drew his belt-sword and cut the ropes with which the tusker was tied to the two guard elephants and sent the two fleeing back into the pen by giving each a hard slap. He then quickly rode the tusker into Travancore. In the confusion Padmanabhan and Kuthira also fled from there.

It was this elephant that later became famous as Kottarakkara Chandrasekharan. Kunjikutty proceeded with the tusker to Thiruvananthapuram to present it to the raja, but when they reached Kottarakkara, the elephant refused to go any further. The raja then went to Kottarakkara and dedicated the elephant to the Shiva temple there.

Chandrasekharan was a highly intelligent and affectionate

elephant, but he had a touch of ferocity in him. And he never forgot a hurt. He was also an expert at throwing stones with his trunk, and if anyone threw stones at him, he would unerringly hit the offender with the very stone he had thrown.

Once when he was standing chained to a tree, he was harassed by a group of urchins, and one of them threw a stone at him. But by the time Chandrasekharan picked up the stone the boy had fled, so he stored the stone in his mouth. He kept it for years, taking it out of his mouth and putting it aside when he fed or drank water, and putting it back afterwards, and was always on the lookout for the boy who threw the stone.

Many years later, when the elephant was leading in a temple procession, he at last saw the boy again, though he had by then grown into an adult. Chandrasekharan then took out the stone from his mouth and unerringly threw it at the man, breaking his leg.

The Making of a Goddess

Many centuries ago there was a wealthy and aristocratic Nair tharavad called Kadamgod in north Kerala. This family was at one time reduced to just one member, a woman, but fortunately she was wonderfully fecund and gave birth to twelve sons and a daughter. The birth of the daughter after so many sons was a particularly joyous event in that matrilineal family, and the child became the darling of all. When her parents died—they died when she was about three—her brothers brought her up with loving care.

The girl was named Makkam, and she grew up into a young woman of great beauty and charm, who was devout, learned, affectionate, gracious and noble-minded, the very pride of her family and community. When she came of age, her brothers found her an ideal match from an equally aristocratic family.

Then the brothers themselves married and brought their wives home. And that was the beginning of the travails of Makkam, for her sisters-in-law were envious of her power and prestige, and resentful of the affection showered on her by her brothers, who did nothing concerning the family without informing her and obtaining her concurrence. Only the youngest sister-in-law remained detached from all this bickering. The malice of the in-laws became more vicious when a boy and a girl were born to Makkam, for that meant that all the family property would go to her children under the matrilineal system.

Makkam was aware of the feelings of her in-laws, and did what she could to assuage their anxieties, and saw to it that they had no cause to complain about any discrimination. Still they remained implacable in their antagonism, and began to pester their husbands with complaints about her. But their pillow-talk had little effect on the men, who remained loyal and affectionate towards their sister. So one day the evil eleven met together secretly and hatched a plot to poison Makkam by bribing the family cook. For this, they pooled 100 rupees each and collected 1100 rupees, a fabulous sum those days. But when they mentioned the plot to the cook, he recoiled in horror. 'Shiva-shiva! This is a horrible sin,' he said, covering his ears with his hands. 'I won't do it even if you give me ten thousand rupees.'

'Alright then,' they said. 'Don't poison Makkam, but serve the poisoned food to us. And when we raise an outcry about it, all you have to do is to say that you added the poison on the orders of Makkam. And we'll give you the promised money.'

The cook reluctantly agreed to this, and the women gave him the poison. A few days later, on a feast day, when all the brothers were together, and the women were sitting down to eat, the cook served them the poisoned rice. Immediately one of the women cried out: 'Why is the rice this colour?' On cue the other women also took up the cry, and charged that the cook had mixed poison in their rice. When this suspicion was confirmed on examination, the brothers gave a thrashing to the cook, who then blurted out that he was told to put poison in the rice by Makkam.

But the ploy did not work. 'I'm totally innocent in this matter,' Makkam declared when confronted with the charge. 'If I'm guilty, may my children and I perish this very moment. If not, the person who told the lie would die.' The moment she spoke these words, the cook went into a convulsion, spitting blood and screaming, 'I lied! I lied!' and fell dead then and there.

This reassured the brothers for the time being, but still a seed of suspicion now lodged in their minds, and this was carefully nurtured by the incessant malicious gossip of their wives. They even accused Makkam of being unchaste, and warned the brothers that she would bring dishonour to the family. Gradually, over several months, they managed to turn the brothers against Makkam, especially by pointing out the grim future that they and their children faced, if all the property went to Makkam and her children.

Evidently then, the best solution to their predicament was to get rid of Makkam and her children. So the brothers, all except the youngest, hatched a conspiracy, and one day invited her to go with them to a festival in a forest temple, saying that it was not good for her to live cooped up in the house all the time. This roused Makkam's suspicion, for they had on several previous occasions refused to take her to the festival even when she had asked them. But Makkam was by now sick of her life in the vicious household, so she took her children and went with the brothers, knowing fully well what was in store for her.

On the way, when they reached a deserted place in the forest, the brothers made Makkam sit under a tree, asking her to rest for a while. There was a deep well there, and looking into it the brothers said, 'Strange! We can see stars in the well. Come and see, Makkam.' And Makkam, thinking that whatever was fated could not be averted, walked over to the well with her children. And as she leaned over it, one of the brothers drew a dagger, stabbed her and the children, and flung them into the well.

The brothers then returned home. But to their horror they saw Makkam standing there in the courtyard, transformed into a fierce, four-armed goddess, performing a horrifying dance of vengeance, as her evil sisters-in-law lay dead around her. The brothers themselves then fell dead, vomiting blood. Only the youngest brother and his wife, who had taken no part in the conspiracy, survived Makkam's holy wrath.

It was thus that Kadamgod Makkam became Makkam Bhagavati, a goddess, immortalized in legend.

One of the most celebrated early modern magicians of Kerala was Cheranalloor Kunju-karthav of the eighteenth century. He belonged to a village about a dozen kilometres north of Ernakulam, and was the head of a prominent local family. But he took no interest in family affairs, and left the management of family properties to his nephews. In fact, he was hardly ever at home, and spent most of his time at the royal court.

Karthav had been given, as a royal favour, the responsibility of collecting the taxes in the region and remitting them to the government, and this again he left to his nephews to handle. But once he was caught in a bind in this matter. There was a delay that year in remitting the tax, so a royal officer arrived at Karthav's home to collect it. But Karthav was unable to pay the dues, as his nephew, who was looking after the tax collection, was not at home at that time. 'Please come tomorrow,' Karthav told the officer. 'My nephew will be back by then. Even if he is not, I'll somehow arrange to make the remittance.'

When the officer arrived the next day, the nephew still

had not returned. Karthav then brought out a chest from the strong-room of the house and counted out from it the money that was due to the government. 'Please check the coins and make sure that they are genuine,' said Karthav. The officer examined the coins and, satisfied with their genuineness, gave Karthav the receipt for the amount received and left.

When the nephew returned and learned that Karthav had paid the tax, he realized that a trick had been played on the royal officer, and he immediately rushed to the treasury in Ernakulam with the tax money to make amends before the fraud was discovered. The officer could not believe what the nephew told him, but was persuaded to bring out the purse that Karthav had given him—and it turned out that what he had taken as money after careful checking were just bits of palm leaves cut in the shape of coins!

Some months later a few princes of the Kochi royal family, hearing of Karthav's reputation, visited him at home and asked him to show them some tricks. So he took them to a pond in the compound. There he made four of his servants stand on the four sides of the pond with loaded muskets, and directed them to shoot at him when he raised his head after diving under water. The servants did as they were told, and this, to the horror of the princes, shattered Karthav's head. Evidently he had made some error in his calculations and had failed to dive back before the shots hit him. Soon the water in the tank turned red with blood, and the corpse of Karthav floated up. The princes felt responsible for the mishap, but as they stood about discussing what to do next, they heard the sound of music from the house. This surprised them, and when they went to investigate, they found Karthav sitting on the parapet of the inner courtyard of the house, calmly playing a veena!

Another day when Karthav was entertaining some guests at home, he asked them what they would like to have to quench their thirst, it being a hot day. 'Tender coconut water would be great,' they said. Karthav hesitated at this. 'My servants are all out on some errand or other just now,' he said. 'But doesn't matter—I'll climb the tree myself.' The guests protested that he should not trouble himself, and said that plain water would do for them. But Karthav insisted on plucking the coconuts.

He tucked up his dhoti and girded it tight around his waist, and effortlessly climbed a coconut tree, plucked a nut from it and threw it down. Then he leapt from the top of the tree to another tree, and kept on leaping from tree to tree like a monkey, plucking coconuts from each. This did not altogether surprise the visitors, for Karthav was reputed to have received special boons from Hanuman, the monkey-god. But in the end he unfortunately missed his hold and fell from the top of a tree with a heavy, crunching thud. When people rushed to him, they found him lying grievously injured and bleeding profusely. He asked them in a dying voice for a drink of water. As they turned to run for water, they found Karthav himself approaching them with a pared coconut! And when they turned to look back at the fallen body, it was gone.

Once a well-known north Indian magician arrived in Ernakulam to perform before the raja, and the raja, along with his retinue and a large number of people, gathered on the shore of the lagoon to watch the performance. And with them was Karthav. The magician walked on water some distance into the lagoon, spread a blanket there and arranged various goods on it. 'Come running,' he called out to the crowd. 'These are great bargains, and they will be gone in a moment.'

The raja then turned to Karthav, who was standing nearby, and asked, 'Can't you go and buy something?'

'With your permission, I'll try,' said Karthav, and leapt on a horse and rode over the water to the magician. But as he approached, the magician, along with all his goods, sank under water, and Karthav had to pull him up and bring him ashore, still riding the horse on water.

It was all an illusion, of course.

❧

A Drummer's Tale

Creative geniuses generally tend to be highly individualistic persons, with scant respect for conventional social values. Such was the character of Mundembilly Krishnan-marar, a drummer of rare virtuosity attached to the royal court in Kochi in the eighteenth century. A singularly testy person, no one liked him, though everyone admired his drumming. Given his talent, he could have made a fortune for himself, but he would not demean himself to curry the favour of the rich and the powerful. He lived exactly as he pleased, doing whatever he liked and saying whatever he thought or felt, without much regard to where he was or who was around.

Krishnan particularly loved to deflate the pride of the pretentious, and often went out of his way to do so. His worst fault in the eyes of others was that he had a mocking tongue, which he at times used cuttingly even against kings. Once when Raja Marthanda Varma of Travancore presented him a bracelet of honour, Krishnan, viewing it as an inadequate reward, impolitely extended his left arm, and when the raja asked him to extend the right arm, he said, 'I'm saving that arm for the time when I would be properly honoured.' So the raja had a second bracelet brought to him, and only then did Krishnan extend his other arm.

The rajas usually overlooked such surly behaviour as pardonable eccentricity in a talented musician. There was no one to match Krishnan in drumming in Kerala at that time. As one distinguished musician remarked, Krishnan did not just play the drum—he romanced the drum. Every time he played a tune, it sounded fresh and new, for Krishnan never repeated himself, but played solely according to the inspiration of the moment, without adhering to any set rules. He was in fact incapable of repeating himself. Once when someone asked him to play what he had played the previous day, he said, 'That's one thing I can't do, for I don't know what I played yesterday, and I don't know what I'm going to play today.'

He had at one time spent a few years travelling around in India, and returned dressed in the style of a Tamilian, wearing a big moustache and his hair rolled into a chignon at the back. The raja of Kochi did not like this, and told him: 'Chignon at the back and moustache are not suited for Malayalees. It's not even proper to enter the temple in this manner. You should change all this.'

And Krishnan said: 'It's my duty to obey your order. But it is your royal duty to satisfy the desires of your dependants. So I think we should reach a compromise in this matter. I'll change my hairstyle and tie the tuft in front, but I should be permitted to keep my moustache.'

And the raja, knowing Krishnan's obstinacy, said, 'As you wish.'

Once the raja granted him two thousand rupees to rebuild his crumbling house. Krishnan considered the amount grossly inadequate, so instead of spending the money on the house, he began building a compound wall around it. When the raja questioned him about it, he said, 'Since the house is inside the compound, I thought I should first secure the compound before starting on the house.' He never completed the wall, of course, nor took up the renovation of the house.

Another time the raja, offended by something that Krishnan had done, ordered him not to step inside the walls of the royal temple where he normally served as a drummer. So that day Krishnan stood on the wall of the temple and drummed, and when people asked him why he was doing that, he said, 'I've been ordered not to enter the temple. But I've not been forbidden from doing my caste duty. That's why I'm standing on the wall and drumming.'

Exasperated by these and other churlish acts of Krishnan, the raja in the end banished him from his kingdom. 'You should never again be seen in my kingdom,' the raja ordered.

And to that Krishnan insultingly responded by requesting the raja to grant him a finger-length of lamp-wick as compensation, implying thereby that the patronage he had received from the raja was worth only that much.

Krishnan scorned material possessions, and never gave any thought to the future. Whatever money he got, he spent it immediately, mostly on women. He was in great demand among connoisseurs all over Kerala, and he used to make a good amount of money touring around, but invariably all that he would have with him when he returned from his tours were only the two dhotis with which he had set out.

ॐ

The Prodigal Priest

There was once a well-known Namboodiri family named Pullamgod in north Malabar. The last head of this family had no children even after many years of marriage, so he performed numerous rites at various temples and pilgrimage centres, and as a result a son was born to him eventually, when he was past sixty. The child was brought up with every tender care by his aged parents. Unfortunately, as the boy grew up, he developed an inordinate fondness for playing cards and gambling, and soon incurred heavy debts. His father, out of his excessive affection for him, quietly paid off all the debts, instead of upbraiding him. The boy thus persisted in his bad habits and continued to accumulate debts, and his father continued to pay them off.

But there was a limit to the forbearance of even this indulgent father, and one day he called his son to him and said, 'My son, what you are doing is not proper. You've squandered a lot of money on something that will not yield any good in this world or in the next. Where will all this end? I'm now over eighty-five years old, and I don't have many more years to live, but think of your own future. You'll one day get married and have your own children, and you will have to provide for them. If you waste all the family wealth in gambling, what'll you do then? That's why I'm anxious that you should change your ways.'

The youth listened thoughtfully to his father. 'You're right,' he said in the end. 'I'll not ever again cause you sorrow in this matter. Whatever has happened, has happened. But I'll ensure that no further debt falls on this family because of me.'

'May god bless you,' said the relieved Namboodiri.

The Namboodiri's optimism was misplaced. What the youth meant was that he would leave his parents and lead an independent life, and not that he would mend his ways.

He left home the very same day. The Namboodiri thought that this was just a peevish act, and that the youth would return home in a couple of days. But as the days stretched into weeks, and the weeks into months, and still his son did not return, the Namboodiri was overcome with grief. He felt that if only he could see his son once again it would not matter even if he lost all his possessions. In this state of mind he finally set out in search of his son.

The youth had gone straight to Thiruvananthapuram on leaving home, for that city was at this time a great centre of all refinements—and of all corruption. Whether it was the Vedas or music or the sciences that one wanted to study, Thiruvananthapuram was the place for it. Equally, it was a great place for gambling, drinking and debauchery. For a Namboodiri it was the best of all places in Kerala to live. If he performed japam (muttered mantras) at the city temple, he was certain to get at least a panam (gold or silver coin) as offering; in addition, there would be special annual gifts from the raja for Onam, the royal birthday, and so on, which would amount to several hundred panams a year. As for his meals, he could have them free at the temple kitchen.

In Thiruvananthapuram the youth continued to indulge in his passion for gambling, borrowing money merrily. It was not difficult for him to get loans, for he was a very personable and charming young man. But this self-indulgent life did not last long. Matters came to a head when he was suspected of stealing some money from the house where he was staying. Though he was not formally accused of the crime, the privileges that he enjoyed at the temple were now stopped on the orders of the raja, and this made it impossible for him to continue to live in the city.

The youth then moved to Suchindram, a temple town near Kanyakumari. There he entered the service of the local temple as a priest and took up his residence with the other priests. This arrangement suited him admirably, for most of the priests there were card players and gamblers, and every night, after completing their temple duties, they sat down to play cards in their lodge. One night when they were thus playing cards, it began to rain heavily, so they had to close all the windows and doors of the room, so that the oil lamp, in the light of which they played, would not blow out. Now our young man was in the habit of chewing paan all the time, so in the middle of the game he had to open the door of the room to spit. As he spat out a mouthful of paan juice, he heard someone ask, 'Is that you, my son?' and recognized his father's voice.

It was on his father, who had come there in search of him, that the youth had unknowingly spat the paan-juice. The sight of his father standing there covered with his spittle suddenly overwhelmed him with grief and regret over the sufferings he had caused to his parents. He then brought a bucket of water, bathed his father and changed his clothes.

Then he fell at his feet in full prostration and prayed, 'Forgive all my misdeeds and bless me.'

The Namboodiri lifted him up and embraced him with tears running down his cheeks. 'Whatever you do,' he said, 'I will never be angry with you, my beloved son.'

That night the youth, lying awake and reviewing his life, decided to totally change his way of life. The next day when the Namboodiri asked him to go home with him, he said that he had taken a vow to spend a year in devotions at the temple, but would return home after that. 'Don't worry, I'll never again revert to my old habits,' he promised.

As promised, he returned home after a year. But when his father suggested that he should get married, he said that he had taken sanyas, and would soon be leaving on a pilgrimage to northern India.

'Then why should we continue to live here?' the Namboodiri asked. 'We will join you in pilgrimage.'

The three of them—father, mother and son—then left for Varanasi, where they spent the rest of their lives.

The Liar Takes All

Raja Rama Varma, who ruled Kochi in the mid-nineteenth century, was a keen patron of literature, and was himself an eminent scholar. He had in his court a number of writers and scholars, the most prominent of whom was Kallur Namboodiri. The raja did not have any great administrative responsibilities at this time, as the state government was run by the diwan under British supervision without much reference to him. He therefore used to spend a good amount of his time with scholars and writers, and holding literary conclaves, at which participants were required to speak on specified topics.

For one such meeting, he set three topics for the courtiers to speak on: 1. Tell a blatant lie and convince everyone that it was absolutely true. 2. Convince all that no one that day had eaten a tastier meal than he had. 3. Get all to agree that he was the luckiest man among them. The winner in each category was offered a purse of 101 panams.

The meeting was set to begin at 11 a.m. and close at 5 p.m. The raja arrived for the meeting at the stroke of eleven, and all the courtiers were already there—all except Kallur

Namboodiri. This surprised everyone, for the Namboodiri was a stickler for punctuality, and usually arrived at meetings well before time. As they were wondering what could have happened to him, he arrived with a downcast face.

'Any problem?' the raja asked solicitously.

'Well . . .' the Namboodiri demurred.

'Tell us.'

'It's a long story,' said the Namboodiri. 'If I go into it, the proceedings here would be delayed.'

'That doesn't matter,' said the raja. 'We are eager to hear what happened to you.'

'If you insist,' said the Namboodiri in a low, dejected tone. 'Sometime back a relative had given me a Nendra-vazha (large banana) sapling. As you know, I love plantains, and as I had only just this one tree, I planted it in the inner courtyard of the house, and we took such good care of it that it grew stout and tall like a palm tree, and its leaves spread over the whole courtyard. And it bore a huge fruit bunch, with twelve clumps of bananas. In about three months, when it began to ripen, I tied a cloth around the bunch, to prevent squirrels from getting at it. Today when I checked it, I found that it had ripened nicely. So I carefully cut down the bunch from the tree and took it to the kitchen. Would you believe it, there were one hundred and twenty-five bananas in the bunch! As I was wondering whether we should eat it fresh or steam it or prepare it some other way, my wife said that it should be made into pradhaman, and I agreed. So she sliced the plantains and fried them in ghee, and then boiled them in milk and sugar, and it turned out to be an excellent dessert—to tell the truth, I had never before tasted such a delicious pradhaman in all my life. But I'm afraid I ate a little too much of it after my meal, so I felt a bit sick later, perhaps because of my old age. So I had to lie down for a while. It was only later that I remembered about this meeting. That's why I got late. I'm sorry.'

'And you didn't send any of the pradhaman to me!' said the raja. 'Whenever you make something special at home, you usually send some to me. Why didn't you do it this time?'

The Namboodiri, embarrassed, averted his eyes.

'Had I known about the pradhaman I would have come to your house for my meal today,' said one of the courtiers at the meeting.

'That's what I was thinking too,' said another, and this chorus was taken up by all. Upon which the Namboodiri went over to where the raja was sitting and took one purse.

'Why are you taking it?' asked the raja.

'You have offered one purse to the person who tells a lie and makes others believe that it is true,' said the Namboodiri. 'What I said about the plantain is an absolute lie. And you all took it to be true. So this purse is mine.'

No one could raise any objection to that. So the Namboodiri took a second purse. And again the raja asked why he took it.

'This purse is for the person who convinces all that he had the tastiest meal today,' said the Namboodiri. 'Since all of you wanted to come to my house to eat pradhaman, this purse is mine.'

Again no one could object to it. Then the Namboodiri took the third purse also. And when questioned about it, he said, 'This purse is for the luckiest man among us. Of all the people here, I've merited two purses. What other proof do you need that I'm the luckiest of all?'

And with that the meeting ended, and the Namboodiri went laughing all the way home, carrying the three purses.

Titbits

The Royal Remedy for Spitting

In the eighteenth century, the narrow lane between the Padbhanabhaswamy and Mithranandapuram temples in Thiruvananthapuram was lined on both sides with the street houses of Namboodiris who had priestly duties in the temples. As the Namboodiris were in the habit of sitting in the veranda of their houses and chewing paan and spitting the juice into the lane, it was difficult for people to walk down the lane without defiling themselves. But no one, not even the rajas, complained about it, out of their respect for the Namboodiris.

Then one day Marthanda Varma, the senior prince of Travancore, thought up a solution to the problem, and had tulasi (holy basil) planted along the length of the lane on both sides. No one, he thought, would spit on this sacred plant.

Sometime later when Rama Varma, the reigning raja, came that way he found the tulasi plants all spattered with the red spittle, and inquired who ordered the tulasi to be planted there and why.

'Appan is yet to learn the ways of the world,' the raja said when he was told why the prince had the tulasi planted there. 'These refined measures will not work in this Kali-yuga, when even Brahmins are thoughtless enough to spit on tulasi.' He then ordered the plants to be removed and had the stocks set up in the street, with a sepoy stationed there with orders to chain anyone who spat on that street.

And the street remained clean thereafter.

Swati Thirunal

Kerala was at one time blessed with several kings of outstanding cultural achievements. One of the most prominent among them was Swati Thirunal of Travancore, who ruled in the first half of the nineteenth century. He was an able administrator, who reformed the kingdom's judicial and tax systems, introduced English education and modern medical practice, established a government engineering department, set up an observatory, undertook major irrigation works, and even took a census of the population of the kingdom. But he is best remembered for his contribution, as a composer, to Carnatic music.

The raja was a liberal-minded and mild-mannered ruler, but there was also something fearsome about his personal appearance, particularly his eyes, which were so fierce that people believed that he was possessed by the spirit of Narasimha, the man-lion incarnation of Vishnu. He usually kept his eyes lowered while speaking to people, and it was said that few people could bear to look into his eyes.

According to legend, a visiting officer of the East India Company once fell in a dead faint when the raja, who had kept his eyes averted during the audience, suddenly looked up at the officer in anger when he made some unreasonable demands. Another time, it is said, when an elephant in a temple procession ran amok and rushed at him, and people around him ran pell-mell, the raja stood his ground, and when the elephant was about to grab him with its trunk, he raised his eyes and looked into the eyes of the elephant, which immediately collapsed, plunging its tusks into the ground.

We do not know what truth there is in all this. But Swati Thirunal was evidently a hands-on ruler, who personally looked into every aspect of government, and was not unduly dependent on his officers. This he once made clear to his diwan in his own inimitable style. When the officer once went on a long leave, he officiously advised the raja to appoint in his place someone senior and experienced, so the government would run smoothly in his absence. The raja agreed to this, but instead of appointing anyone in the place of the diwan, he directed a clerk to place an old and worn broom on the officer's chair. When the diwan returned and found the broom on his seat, and learned why it was there, he got the message.

The Illusionist

One of the most renowned Kathakali exponents of the eighteenth century was Parameswara-chakyar. One day when he was on the beach in Thiruvananthapuram, the pet dog of an English officer ran barking at him, and fearing that it might bite him, the Chakyar pretended to pick up a stone and throw it at the dog. So realistic was the act that the dog ran away whining as if it was hit. The Englishman also thought that the dog was hit, and, on learning that the man who threw the stone was in the royal service, he immediately took the complaint to the raja, who was at this time in his beach house.

The raja then called the Chakyar and sought an explanation from him. The Englishman was not convinced when the Chakyar said that he only pretended to throw the stone. Upset about this, the Chakyar picked up a granite stone lying there and, assuming wrath, swung it at the Englishman. The man immediately lurched back and fell, holding his head. When it was found that the stone was not actually thrown, it convinced everyone that no stone was thrown at the dog either.

A Tale of Two Swords

There were very few people who ever got the better of Sakthan Thamburan, but Kunjikutty, the chief minister of Travancore once did. Hearing of the extraordinary skills of Kunjikutty as a strategist and soldier, Sakthan once wrote to the Travancore raja expressing a desire to see him. The raja sent Kunjikutty to Kochi, but warned him, 'Sakthan is simple-minded but hot-tempered, and when roused will do anything. Be careful with him.'

So it was with some trepidation that Kunjikutty presented himself at the court of Sakthan. When he made his obeisance, the raja held out his sword and asked, 'See this?'

'Eran!' acknowledged Kunjikutty courteously. 'Your slave also has a small one with him,' he said and pulled out and showed his belt-sword.

'Give it to me,' said the raja.

'May I request Your Majesty to give me your sword first?'

Kunjikutty received the raja's sword reverently with both hands, bowing low.

'Now give me your sword,' said the raja.

'I'm sorry, Your Majesty,' said Kunjikutty. 'This sword was presented to me by my king. I cannot give it to anyone.'

'Then give me back my sword,' said the raja.

'I'm sorry, Your Majesty,' said Kunjikutty. 'I esteem you no less than I esteem my own king, so it won't be proper for me to return the sword with which you honoured me. Nor is it proper for you to take back what you have presented.'

The raja was delighted with the cunning of Kunjikutty.

'You're not Kunjikutty (little baby),' he said laughing. 'You're Anakutty (baby elephant).'

A True Prediction

Sakthan Thamburan's dictatorial ways were not liked by his cousins who, according to the matrilineal system followed by the Kochi royal family, were next in the line of succession. Once, when the raja was camping in Thrissur, they called a renowned astrologer to the Tripunittura palace to predict when the raja would die. The astrologer made his calculations and wrote down the year, month, day and time when the raja would die.

Somehow the raja came to hear of this, and he had the astrologer seized when he was passing through Thrissur.

'I hear that you have given in writing when I'll die,' said the raja to the astrologer when he was brought before him.

'I've stated what my calculations indicated,' said the astrologer.

'Your prediction will not come true,' said the raja. 'But I'll make a prediction now, and it will certainly come true—you'll die before sundown today.'

He then called his captain and ordered him to tie up the astrologer, and have him beaten to death before the sun set that day.

The Raja and the Oracle

One of the most popular temple festivals of Kerala is the Thrissur Pooram, which was introduced by Sakthan Thamburan in the eighteenth century. Previously the area around the temple was a dense teak forest through which people were afraid to pass even during daytime. It was Sakthan who cleared the land

and laid out the processional way there. But there was resistance to the clearing of the land from the oracle of the nearby Bhagavati temple. One day, while the raja was supervising the clearing of the jungle, the oracle arrived there in a state of frenzy, as if possessed by the goddess, and declared, 'This is my father's jada (matted hair); you shall not cut it down.'

The raja was nonchalant. 'Where were you and your father when Tipu Sultan entered the temple and threw out the idol?' the raja scoffed. 'Don't talk nonsense. I've decided to clear this place. You better leave quietly.'

'You playing with me, son? Watch!' said the oracle, and began striking his head with his ritual sword, drawing blood, but causing no serious hurt, as the sword was blunt.

'Your sword is not sharp—here take mine,' said the raja and forced his own sword on the oracle and slammed it into his head, cleaving it. The raja then calmly proceeded with the clearing of the land.

A Pardon Too Late

Once when Sakthan Thamburan jailed a rich Thiyya for the minor offence of polluting a Namboodiri, the Thiya's relatives sought the help of an influential courtier to get him released by presenting him with a purse. The raja came to hear about this, so he secretly ordered one of his officers to shoot the Thiyya dead just when the courtier arrived to see him. When the courtier appeared and began pleading for the release of the Thiyya, the raja heard a gunshot, and, pretending innocence, asked his officers what that shot was. They told him that it was the Thiyya being executed according to his order of the previous day. 'Oh yes, I forgot,' he said. 'What a pity, if only you had come to me yesterday I could have released the man.'

Vikata-Saraswati

In medieval Kerala, Namboodiris were generally men of learning, but there were a few among them who lived solely by their wits. One such person was Muttuss Namboodiri of Vaikam. He had hardly any scriptural knowledge, but was wonderfully inventive and witty, and was said to be possessed by Vikata-Saraswati, the naughty aspect of the goddess of learning.

It was a custom among scholars in Kerala to present dramatized lectures on sacred texts during major temple festivals, and this was a source of income for them. Since our hero did not know any texts, he merely dressed up and stood behind a lighted lamp pretending to offer lectures, and since no one went to listen to him, he could get away with the sham and collect the fee given to lecturers. But one day a man, intending to expose the Namboodiri, went and stood before him. This obliged the Namboodiri to recite something, which he promptly did:

> *Ghataa pataa ghata-pataa ghatapaatapataa*
> *Bhataa chataa chata-chataa hata chaata-chaataa*
> *Mooddaa kataa katakataa katakaata kaataa*
> *Kutaa kutaa kutukutaa kutiyaatikutaa.*

He then went on to explain the nonsense stanza according to his whimsy. When the listener asked from which text he had taken the verse, and to repeat the explanation once more, the Namboodiri flared up, 'God! Am I your disciple to recite whatever you ask! Begone!' he cried indignantly.